PROMISES AND PIXIE DUST

ELLE MADISON
ROBIN D. MAHLE

WHISKEY & WILLOW
publishing

For our Drifters and Wanderers
You helped choose the story and the title — so this is all your fault.

This is the story of a girl the size of a thumb, who was born from the blossom of a rare tulip.
At least, that's the way Mama always told it, and who's to say she's wrong?
After all, if I didn't come from a flower, where did I come from?
And is there anyone out there like me?

1

LINA

It was good to be back.

Foam tickled my nose as I peered down into the sparkling chalice on the bar. The glass was very nearly my height, but that didn't matter to me one bit—not when most things were made for people so much bigger than me.

"Careful there, little lady." The voice came from a man I'd never seen in here before, sitting a couple of barstools down.

I studied his friendly face and noticed the glossy look of inebriation in his eyes. Maybe he didn't mean *little* as an insult, but he had no idea how unnecessary his warning was.

I smiled back at him over the rim of my glass, but someone else responded for me.

"Don't worry, Breldor. Lina can hold her liquor better than your average Ogre," my friend Vale said, from the other side of the bar. Then he glanced at the stool behind me, red flushing into his cheeks. "No offense, Wigbert."

"None taken," the kind ogre assured him.

The man simply nodded before taking his drinks back to his booth. Vale gave me a small wink before topping off my glass and heading back to the kitchens. I almost swore I heard the hearts of several girls break at his departure. I knew that most of them came to this tavern for a glimpse of him, if not for his fantastic cooking skills alone.

When it was his sister's turn at the bar, the smiles and attention didn't lessen. Neira and Vale were cut from the same perfect cloth; stunning creatures with raven-colored hair that contrasted starkly against their porcelain skin and hazel eyes. Their younger siblings shared these gorgeous looks, as well, and thus, all four were widely recognized around town.

Taking a sip of my ale, I couldn't deny the slight jealousy that rose up inside of me as I watched the room watch them for their beauty, and not for their oddities. *What I wouldn't give to know other people who look more like me.*

I'd never seen someone as small as me in the village— and I'd never heard of anyone like me outside of it. As far as I knew, I was the only one of my kind.

When Mama was alive, none of that seemed to matter. But now...

I took a deep breath, allowing the heady scents of whiskey and roasted meats to transport me to a happier time in my life. One when I would spend a few nights a week here at the tavern with my closest friends. One where I wasn't mourning or avoiding those same people for fear of breaking down all over again.

By my fourth pint, I was feeling better than I had in ages. The apple ale dulled the back spasms that had assaulted me for years, and it even soothed that ache in my chest that came whenever I thought of Mama.

It's just the distraction I need.

The familiar clinking of glass and metal ricocheted as Neira poured tankards of ale, whiskey, and cider for the eager customers, and their coins hit the bar in payment.

"Hey, Lina's back!" A few of the elves called over to me as they made their way to a shared booth with a group of orcs, something you would never see outside of this tavern.

I waved and smiled. The Poisoned Apple Tavern was a safe haven for all of us *misfits*. For anyone who the High Queen of Floriend hadn't deemed *human enough*.

As far as I knew, it was the one place in the world where there was an unspoken truce, no matter where you came from; Orcs, Elves, Men, Ogres, and one thumb-sized girl could all meet up, share a meal, and know that the man next to him wasn't an enemy.

And I knew all of them, for the most part. Each of them had been there for me during Mama's funeral. Every person here, everyone I'd ever known, had shown up and offered their condolences.

Everyone but *him*.

I pushed the thought away as Neira approached, bringing me another pint and a plate of fried vegetables with my favorite dipping sauce. My mouth was already watering when she set the plate down in front of me. An unexpected squeak escaped my lips as she pulled out a slice of apple pie with the crumbly sweet topping I loved from the cooling tray, and added it to my plate.

Not a slice for someone my size, but a regular one. A

slice I could sleep on if I didn't have plans to devour it whole.

"It's on the house," she said, walking away before giving me a chance to argue.

"I'll have whatever she's having." A feminine voice came from behind me as she strode up to the bar.

Neira smiled at her and handed her a slice of pie before a furry hand reached out and scratched at the counter.

"One for Frankie, too?" Neira asked and the girl smiled.

"Yes, please."

My attention went back to my plate as the tempting smells wafted up toward me, intoxicating as they were. It wasn't long before I decided that dessert would be first this evening.

Sighing, I took a bite of the pie, practically groaning with delight. I knew I was glowing bright orange. I didn't care. Each bite was better than the last.

The crispy, buttery crust, and sweet cinnamon-apple filling made me momentarily forget every negative feeling I'd ever had, and it wasn't long before I'd eaten well over half of it.

At least I can still find comfort in food.

"It's good to see you again." Neira's voice drifted down from her spot behind the bar. "This place hasn't been the same without you. You're beginning to look more like yourself again, you know. For that matter, you appear to be eating more like yourself again, too." She winked, but I could hear the relief in her voice. "Should I tell Vale to make more?"

I mockingly rolled my eyes, but then nodded, making Neira laugh.

"It does feel good to be back, though," I eventually added, with a smile.

Neira's kind eyes were hopeful and simultaneously filled with the sort of pity that made my heart ache. An all-too-brutal reminder that it had only been just a few months since I'd lost my mother.

Taking another long slurp of the ale, I peered up at my friend.

"Is it wrong? To be happy again, I mean."

My gaze darted back down to my hand around the straw as it faded from its usual shade of pink to a soft blue. The very color I had been for nearly a year now—ever since we got the news that Mama was sick. Then, as she worsened. And finally, when she died.

Several silent moments passed between us. When I looked back up, Neira's eyes had darkened, and she'd paused in her cleaning of a few whiskey bottles. She was staring at the wall, memories of her own mother's death probably coming back to haunt her.

Shaking her head, she set down the amber-filled glass and moved closer, leaning her elbows on the bar before speaking again.

"No, Lina. It's not wrong. And your mother wouldn't want you to grieve forever." She held out a hand, and I grasped her finger. "The pain will come and go, but you honor her memory more with your joy than you do with your tears. She would want you to find your happiness again."

"Here, here," Wigbert said from behind me, raising his glass in agreement.

Neira and I smiled back at him.

They're right. Mama wasn't one to dwell on the past.

She'd taught me to hope and to move forward. And as difficult as that seemed, I owed it to her to at least try.

"Here, here," I agreed with the ogre, noting the way my speech slurred ever so slightly.

A groan sounded to my left, and I grinned.

"Princess." Wigbert addressed Piper with a small bow of his head.

She nodded back before rapping her knuckles on the bar to signal that she needed a drink.

Dark circles lined her violet eyes, and her purple satin dress was slightly disheveled. The tiny dragon curled in her lap was only a shade darker than her gown, so camouflaged I would have missed him if it weren't for the steady rise and fall of his breathing.

"Her Ladyship is still at it, then?" Neira asked, taking in her appearance while she filled a shot glass with Piper's favorite whiskey.

The princess downed it in one go before motioning for another round.

"You have no idea," she grumbled, as Neira filled the glass once more. Piper demolished that shot, as well, before resting her face in her hands.

Before anything else could be said, the door to the kitchens swung open and Vale walked through. Piper suddenly sat up straighter, swallowing hard and smoothing out her silky golden locks. Her perfect features hardened as her eyes followed him across the room to tend to newly seated customers.

Neira and I gave each other a questioning look before staring at her. Piper pretended to ignore us, of course, but the way she was petting her dragon was a little too casual.

"I don't want to talk about *Her Ladyship* right now, or about anything else."

I opened my mouth to tell them what I had spent ages planning when the bell above the tavern door jingled.

Even though I'd specifically come here tonight to speak to him, my heart hammered within my ribcage the moment my eyes met Edrich's.

2

EDRICH

I knew Lina was here before I even saw her.

Ever since we were kids, I could practically sense her in a room. She may as well have been shooting off beams of sunshine like a beacon, leading me directly to her.

Even when I don't want to see her.

Sure enough, there she was, standing—or swaying, anyway—on top of the polished oak bar. At twelve centimeters high, she was barely taller than the tiny ornate cup she drank from, and not half as high as the tankard of the man next to her.

I brought my fingers to the bridge of my nose. This was the last thing I wanted to deal with tonight, but I knew I couldn't avoid her forever after her mother's funeral. *Not that I had seen her then, either.* I still wasn't sure what would have been worse; facing every single demon in my past and confronting the death of one of the few decent people in the world, or what I had actually wound up doing the day of the funeral.

"You gonna stand in the door all day, mate? I'm getting soaked out here." Atesh's voice sounded behind me, happier than he had a right to be after what we'd just done.

But then, he had a few years of experience on me. Enough time to learn to leave the missions behind when you were finished with them. *Or maybe he's just better at ignoring that constant gnawing sense of guilt than I am.*

I sighed.

Maybe someday I would be able to shut the screams out, too, but today they seemed determined to keep me company to punish me.

And rightly so.

I shifted out of the way, allowing him room to walk around me out of the rain and into the tavern, making a beeline for the bar.

Or, I suspected, the striking woman behind it.

"Edrich!" Lina's voice was surprisingly loud for such a tiny person, pulling me out of my own head, and back to the crowded bar around me.

I knew she came here on occasion, but she usually left before night fell. I knew this because I made sure to ask after a couple of accidental run-ins. I didn't like seeing her when I wasn't prepared for it.

"Lina." I said her name with markedly less excitement than she had shown, covering the distance between us in a few short strides. "What are you still doing here?"

The question was for her, but the hulking creature next to her with coarse, olive skin decided to move as well. Ogres were deceptively mild and unfailingly polite, something I could have done without right about now.

I didn't want to sit by her. I didn't even want to be in this bar with her. I just wanted to drink enough ale to forget the sound of a woman pleading for her children's safety, knowing it would do no good.

"Thank you, Wigbert!" Lina called after the ogre, her pink skin brightening with sincerity, before she turned to me. "And actually, I was waiting for you."

I removed my wet cloak and signaled for an ale to fortify me for the conversation I could have gone my entire life without having.

"Look, Lina, I'm sorry I couldn't make—"

"It's all right." But her sparkling rose-gold skin and blue-green eyes dimmed. "I got your note."

"I'm sorry." Princess Piper, a girl with golden-blonde hair and bright, purple eyes peeked around the ogre, and I could pretty well guess from her expression that she was not remotely sorry about whatever she was about to say. *Typical royal.* "Did you just say you sent a *note*? To her *mother's funeral*? I hope you at least sent flowers with it."

A purple reptilian head stretched up from her lap, eyeing me like it was affirming her indignation. I took another long drink before I could say something I would regret.

This day just keeps getting better and better.

"You can't expect a man to think of flowers, Piper." The familiarity of the new voice surprised me. I turned to see a curvy woman with skin the color of tree bark, and eyes to match, standing on the other side of me.

"She's lucky he sent a note." Jessie looked at me out of the corner of her eye.

There was a slight undercurrent there, but that was fair. I wasn't great about keeping up with people... even people I had been on dates with. She briefly put a hand on my shoulder in a gesture of peace, then turned to order another round from Vale.

She's clearly nicer than I deserve, anyway.

I turned my attention back to Lina in time to see her skin flashing between her usual rose-gold color and a deep, forest green. *Is she going to vomit?* It had been a lot of ale for such a tiny person.

But her color evened out and she spoke over whatever response Piper was muttering.

"That's not why I was looking for you," she said, before hiccupping.

"Then why?" I asked.

"Because I need your help with something," she answered, taking another sip of her enormous drink.

For some inexplicable reason, I expected her to make a face like when we were kids getting into her mother's stash of strawberry wine, but of course, she had been well past drinking age for a few years now. I just never stayed at the farm long enough to see her for more than a few minutes, let alone grab a pint with her.

So, she had found me instead.

"With what?" *What can she possibly need from me at this point?*

Hadn't I given her enough in the years my entire life revolved around her? Not that she understood that. Not that she ever would.

She deflated a little at my abrupt tone, and I used the momentary distraction of Vale sliding another pint down the bar to pretend not to notice.

"Because you are a soldier, and I have need of one," she finally answered.

I nearly choked on the swig of ale I had taken, coughing a few times before, clearing my throat.

"Is that what you think? That I'm a soldier?" I laughed, but there was no joy in the sound.

She was so sheltered, even now, even by my own family. *They know perfectly well how I make my living.*

"Yes," she said, uncertainly.

Her skin darkened to a deeper pink, the color of embarrassment. She reined it in quickly, though, her eyes roaming from the falconer's perch on my wrist to the sword at my belt.

"Yes." She said it more firmly this time.

I shook my head, my eyes searching skyward — like the ceiling held any more answers than the drink in front of me did. I drained my mug in one long draught before turning back to face her, and I realized I was just as bad as the rest of them, an enabler for this completely unrealistic existence she lived in.

Because I couldn't quite bring myself to tell her the truth.

"Yeah, Lina. I'm a soldier." After all, it sounded better than *Huntsman*.

3

LINA

Wiping away a few imaginary crumbs from my sundress gave me something else to focus on for the moment. I wasn't sure why I was so insistent on him coming along. Why I thought I needed him, or why I thought if we could just get away—just the two of us—that things could be different.

Maybe I was holding on to a memory of a man who no longer existed. Of a relationship that neither of us wanted or needed. But when I looked up at his face, the dark circles under his eyes, the fierceness of his gaze, the clear lines of exhaustion in his expression... all the broken parts of him that reminded me he still had a heart, I couldn't help but hope.

So instead of taking offense at his usual clipped tones, I only sighed audibly. "Well, I can see you're wearing your pleasant pants again today."

His eyebrows rose, what might have been a smile trying to peek through his dark expression. "How could I resist, when they go so well with my somber shoes?"

A startled laugh bubbled out of me, at least until the girl who'd put her hand on his shoulder earlier began speaking to him again.

Well. He had no trouble smiling where *she* was concerned.

She kissed his cheek before walking back to her table, and I felt my skin go green all over again. Even if she hadn't been gorgeous, her chestnut locks a perfect contrast to his sandy blonde, she was his size. *Something I will never be.*

"Lina, did you hear me?" Edrich's voice pulled me back to reality. "And why are you green again? What's wrong?"

I looked down at the deep, shining green that was pulsing under my skin, offset even more by the pale, purple fabric of my dress, and tried to come up with something to explain away the color.

"It's nothing." *Very convincing.* I looked anywhere but at his face.

"Are you sure?"

"Of course," I lied.

"Of course." His tone was overly agreeable.

I ignored him, taking another long gulp of ale. *You're a mess, Lina. Get it together.* I could feel, more than see, my skin changing into a kaleidoscope of colors, emotions darting through me faster than I could control.

Emerald. Amethyst. Ruby. All on repeat.

I focused on the little things. The sound of laughter in the tavern, the smell of pie wafting in from the kitchens, the way the leather straps of my shoes made a crisscross pattern — anything to distract myself. Anything to calm myself.

Edrich shook his head when I didn't say anything else,

then stared at the ceiling. The silence that stretched between us was palpable.

Thankfully, a familiar voice interrupted the lull.

"Lina, Darling, are you sure you want this one?" Piper tilted her chin toward Edrich. "Surely, you could find a more congenial *soldier*."

A loud huff of air came from Edrich as his jaw clenched.

"Speaking of congenial, shouldn't you be with your *Lord* right about now, Piper?" Edrich signalled for another ale, not bothering to look in her direction.

Piper's cheeks reddened. Everyone in the tavern knew that she snuck out of the Estate where she was supposed to be staying to get to know her fiancé because his entire family was insufferable.

Piper shifted on her stool so that she was looking directly at Edrich. Red blossomed in her cheeks and her eyes narrowed. When her lips parted, I panicked. I tried to think of something to say that would prevent this all from escalating, but I didn't have nearly enough time to think my words through.

"I want him!" I blurted out. "I mean, I need him...err... I want him with me when I go find the fairies." *Fantastic.* My attempt to cover had me sounding like a crazy person before I even had the chance to explain.

While the rest of the tavern went about their evening, my friends all stopped and stared, their jaws hanging open in shock.

"Wha—" Neira started and stopped, her attention having been ripped away from the handsome soldier who'd arrived with Edrich.

Even Piper was speechless.

I was ready for their surprise. I knew that would wear off, eventually, as they understood why I needed to do this. What I hadn't expected was Edrich's carefully blank expression; the way his knuckles went white around his mug of ale.

Whatever small bit of warmth and life had entered his face for a few minutes was gone now. I prepared myself for his onslaught of words, but only a single word escaped his clenched jaw.

"No."

"Yes," I said back, and he huffed a sigh. "I've thought about it for a long time now, and it's something I need to do."

For years, I'd dreamed of finding people like me. People my size, a world I could thrive in. *And now that Mama is gone... what else is keeping me here?*

I swallowed hard before continuing.

"And I'd like you to come with me."

Edrich opened his mouth to speak, then closed it again. When he finally got something out, it was just a repeat of that single word, again.

"No." It sounded more like a denial of my entire plan, than an actual response.

"If this isn't something you're up for, if it isn't something you want to do, I understand. I'm sure I can find someone else to accompany me. But either way, I *am* going."

Piper and Neira were silent as they watched our showdown, Edrich shaking his head in disbelief, and me looking up at him with far more hope than I should've allowed myself to have.

When minutes had passed and he still didn't respond, I

stood straighter, trying to will a confidence into myself that I didn't ever feel around him anymore.

"I'm leaving in two days. If you want to come with me, meet me here at dawn," I said, with a forced, casual smile.

Edrich downed the rest of his ale and stood, the scraping of his chair ringing out louder than any other noise in the bar.

"No," he repeated, with finality. "Even *if* the fairies still exist, the forest is no place for you. People bigger and stronger than you walk into that forest and don't come back out."

My eyes widened, and I stared at him incredulously as he pulled out two copper coins from his pocket and set them down on the bar.

"I know the stories. I know the risk, and that it's a long shot." I fought to keep my voice even. "You don't have to believe in the fairies, Edrich, but is it so much for you to ask to believe in me?"

Piper cleared her throat and motioned for another round, while Neira busied herself to provide it, giving us a moment of privacy.

He didn't look at me when he responded, his voice tired... and maybe even a little bit sad. "I'm not like you, Lina. I can't make myself believe in something that isn't true. So yes, it is a lot to ask that I just set reason aside and believe that you will magically make it through the most dangerous forest in the world unscathed, that you'll find your way to creatures no one has seen or heard from in a thousand years."

A bitter huff of air escaped my lips, but I tried one more time. "Can you honestly not understand at all why I need to do this?"

Edrich finally turned back to face me, his eyes meeting mine.

"No, I can't say that I do understand why you feel the need to risk your life chasing a legend. And mine, apparently." He ran his hand over his eyes, his features somewhere between exasperation and pleading. "Just... stay here, at the farm, with your animals and your flowers, where it's peaceful and safe. Where *you're* safe."

Leaving no room for further conversation, he grabbed his cloak and left the tavern. The man he'd arrived with, the one who had been pining over Neira, followed after him.

The only sound I heard was the chiming bells ringing out over the door while I stared after his shadow.

I wondered if he heard how condescending that sounded. *Stay safe, Lina. You're too tiny and weak to go off into the forest, Lina.*

A heat wave rolled through me, and I was certain that my skin had once again deepened to ruby.

I drank down the rest of the ale quickly, as every look, every word, every sigh raced through my mind. A twitch of pain jolted down my spine, and I tried to breathe through it, counting slowly until it passed.

Maybe that was the worst part. As much as I'd implied that I could do it on my own, I knew full well that I couldn't. Not really. *Not like this.*

"You all right, Lina?" Neira eventually asked, bringing me back to the present.

I looked up to see her and Piper silently waiting.

"I'm fine," I said, pushing my chalice toward Neira and burying my anger. "It's probably time for me to head home, too."

"Oh, no. Not yet, you're not." Piper added with a shake of her head. "Not until you tell us the full story. Why the sudden urge to run off to find the fairies? And why would you want to take that brooding oaf with you?"

Her question stung for more reasons I cared to admit at that moment. *He wasn't always brooding*, I wanted to say. But I was tired of defending him tonight, and tired of thinking about the person he used to be, when he had made it so clear who he was now. Instead, I answered her first question.

"I need to know where I came from. I need to know if I really am the only one of my kind."

Piper rested her hand next to me, and I leaned into it.

"As much as we can, Lina, we understand," she said, softly.

"We really do," added Neira. "But how do you know if you'll even find them? If they even still exist?"

"I don't. But I have to try. I need to know if I'm the only one of my kind."

I need to know if I'll be alone for the rest of my life.

4

EDRICH

Atesh followed me outside where the rain had finally stopped.

"Listen, go with the girl or don't, but take a few days off either way. You need them, and, honestly, so do I. Besides, we can still hope that last mission was the final one from *her*..." His voice trailed off, and I wondered, not for the first time, if he was regretting taking the queen's deal all those months ago as much as I did.

But for better or worse, we were a team, and the man had never actually admitted he wanted to take time away. The least I could do was make it easy on him.

"All right, sure."

He smiled then, white teeth flashing against deep, brown skin. It was more than I could manage. I just gave him a nod before turning back toward my horse. I whistled before I mounted Hobgoblin, waiting a few minutes for the answering screech from my gyrfalcon, Pepper.

Once I knew she could find me, I climbed onto my

warhorse and headed toward the last place I felt like being right now.

Home.

It was harder and harder to face my family after every job, and this last one had been worse than most. More than that, though, I knew what they would say about Lina.

You have to stop her.

Or, worse, *You have to go with her.*

And I didn't particularly want to do either. It would be nice if something in my life could be about... not her. Anything but her, really.

But as I rode up to the quiet cottage where I had spent most of my life to find my parents sitting on the front porch in their wooden rocking chairs, healthy and alive and happy, I knew I wouldn't have it any other way.

"Your father is dying." The small man had come out of nowhere, stopping me on my walk to check the fences.

Well, man was a stretch. He looked more like a garden gnome, with green skin and eyes the color of burnished gold.

"I know," I said back, proud of the way my voice didn't shake.

"I can save him." The man pulled a clear vial out of his pocket, full of a swirling, oily substance. "It's not a cure, but it will keep the sickness at bay for as long as he takes it."

I couldn't take my eyes off the first thing that had felt like hope in months. But...

"We don't have much money."

"That's all right. I don't deal in coin."

"Then what do you deal in?" I scrunched up my face in confusion.

He splayed his hands out to the side. "Favors."

"Anything," I breathed, too desperate for wariness. Too desperate to ask what he could possibly need from a poor village

boy, when there were countless people in the world who owed him favors.

"There's a girl on the small farm next to you. A very special girl. I want you to make it your mission in life to keep her safe."

Whatever I had been expecting, it wasn't that. If anything, it seemed a relatively mild favor to give in exchange for a life.

"Why would you care about Lina?" Of course, I knew her name.

Everyone in town knew about the thumb-sized girl, but I had also spent time at her farm with her. She was funny, and not half as strange as people thought, once you got to know her.

"That's not important. All that matters to you is, as long as she's safe and healthy, so is your father." The man smiled to reveal teeth the same color as his eyes. "So, do we have a deal?"

I couldn't say yes fast enough back then. I didn't think to ask how long this would go on—how long my father's life would be held over our heads—even with Lina well into adulthood. He didn't give me time, really. He handed me the cure, then instructed me to tell no one outside my family what we had spoken about.

Though I suppose even if I had been given time for all of those questions, it hardly would have mattered. Not to my ten year-old self, and not now. *My father's life is more than worth it.*

My family was confused when I told them what I had done, but grateful. After all, how hard could it be to keep one tiny girl safe? And maybe it wouldn't have been if Lina had been a different sort.

But, no. She was always trying to befriend spiders and climb onto birds, and she took naps in the flowers the horses liked to run through.

And now this. I rubbed at my temples.

"What's wrong?" Eddard didn't even give me time to dismount before he grilled me, but then, patience had never been my brother's strong suit. "Did you get the medicine?"

The question had been laced with fear ever since we found out who our savior was. Rumplestiltskin was not a man, or troll, to be trifled with. But, he had never gone against his word, either. Nor had he ever answered any of my questions about why he cared so much if Lina lived or died.

"Yes." I handed the vial over to him.

I had picked it up at the same place I always did, from a woman who refused to tell me how she procured it, even when I offered her the substantial amount of blood money I had received in exchange for my most recent job. My family needed the coin, but not as much as they needed to be out from under the weight of my obligation.

Especially when the weight of that burden fell on them, as making the money they needed to survive had fallen on me.

But it didn't matter. For ten years, the woman had given the vial to me, and me alone, and only once she had received word from Rumplestiltskin.

"Then what is it?" my brother asked.

"What is what?" I countered.

"Your face." He gave me a knowing look, and I shouldered past him.

"This is just my face, Eddard," I lied, walking toward our house.

"Is this about Lina offering us the farm?" he asked, quietly, holding out a hand to stop me before we reached our parents.

"She did what?" I asked, sharply.

"She asked us to manage the farm for her," he said. "I thought she told you."

"No, she didn't." But it meant she was serious about her plan, if she had found someone else to look over her mother's beloved farm.

"So what's upsetting you, then?"

Well, what the hell. *He's going to find out eventually*.

"She wants to go into the forest, to find the fairies. Because she thinks *she's* a fairy." It was ludicrous, hearing it out loud. Though nothing about Lina had ever made sense.

"Who's to say she isn't? It's not like anyone remembers what they look like, and she has to have come from somewhere." He echoed my reluctant thoughts before cocking his head like the perceptive bastard he was. "What bothers you so much about that?"

"She wants me to go with her."

He eyed me for a long moment, like he saw far more than he should at only sixteen years-old. Then again, I had left home at only a year older than he was, now.

"Well, you have to, don't you?" he finally responded. "She'll get herself hurt, or worse, in those woods."

I looked at where my father had raised a hand in greeting, at the vial my brother was still holding; the medicine keeping the man who had given us everything alive.

Then, I pictured tiny little Lina in the forest full of venomous insects and all other manner of deadly creatures, half of which she'd probably try to make friends with, and I sighed.

"Yeah, I guess I do."

LINA

Now that every last detail of the farm was squared away, there was nothing left for me to do but to move forward—to move on.

I distracted myself by touching up the paint on my hedgehog's nails. It was a dusty rose color, and it matched the paint on mine. Maggie grinned and sat still while I finished, practically drifting back to sleep as I worked. She'd always loved when I did this. It was as relaxing to her as it was to me.

Soon, her snores filled the room.

It was just as well. We had a long journey ahead of us, and she needed the rest. Once I was done, I stood to stretch, and a cramp by my spine reminded me that I needed to reapply my medicine before we left.

Uncle had supplied us with the strange ointment for as long as I could remember—peppermint and eucalyptus, and something earthy I couldn't quite place. He said it was common among people my size.

People my size.

When I'd asked him about it later, he insisted that it was something he'd heard from a healer from far away... someone who had encountered another person like me. The mere idea that there was someone else out there like me was wonderful. I was enraptured with the thought for a whole minute before he crushed my dreams as they formed.

"They are long since gone, my child. There is no use trying to find them."

Still, the idea never fully left me. Mama indulged me and found every book, rumor, tale, and anecdote she could on little people, fairies, sprites, and more.

Uncle wasn't happy when he found out, but Mama had convinced him it was fine.

I closed my eyes and could see them before me, plain as day. I could practically hear their voices... Wringing my hands and squeezing my eyes shut tight, I tried to block out the pain and worry that had been plaguing me. I'd lost Mama, and I hadn't heard from Uncle since her funeral.

"He's a nomad, Lina. You're used to him being away for long periods of time." I whispered the assurance to myself, though I didn't believe a word of it.

Because he'd never been gone *this* long...

Is he dead, too?

I shook my head as if that would erase the dread. That wasn't a thought I could entertain now, or ever. I'd had too many goodbyes, too many worries. Glancing around the dark, empty bedroom broke my heart enough that I couldn't indulge some awful thing that might not even be true.

Looking over my checklist one more time, I marked off each item I'd already packed away. There were only a handful of things left, and I busied myself with folding up a few dresses and tunics with leggings, my nightdress, extra unmentionables, toiletries, snacks, and of course, my map.

It wasn't fancy. In fact, it was barely legible, but it would have to do. All of the research I'd done led me to believe that the ancient fairy kingdom still existed, and it wasn't leagues away as Uncle had made it seem.

It was just through the Enchanted Forest.

I took a deep breath and prayed I was right, that this wasn't just some fool's errand that would lead me to more questions than answers.

But it's a risk I'm willing to take.

I wasn't sure if I would ever come back here... or that I even wanted to. I couldn't hide here anymore, wallowing in a life that no longer existed.

No, I needed to make a new life for myself. *Or at least try.*

A rooster crowed, pulling me from my thoughts.

"Frolicking centaurs! I'm going to be late," I realized, with a start.

I ran back up to the window frame to wake Magnolia as gently as I could.

"It's time, Maggie," I whispered.

She stretched and yawned before wobbling to her newly manicured paws with a small nod.

We made our way down the built-in staircase from the window to the floor, winding our way toward the front door.

I looked back at the only home I'd known and sighed. In my mind, I painted a portrait of each detail—each speck of dust, each rickety floorboard, of each memory of the only home I could remember.

A small grunt sounded behind me as Maggie's snout rested under my hand. I took her subtle reminder and used the pulley system to close the massive door behind us.

"Goodbye, Mama," I said, pressing a kiss to my palm and resting it against the frame.

Maggie and I made our way down the path to the wagon that our farmhand had readied for us.

"Are you sure you don't want me to come with you? At least to the tavern?" he asked, bleary-eyed.

"No, but thank you, Stephen. The Adlers should be here later today. If you need anything, just let them know," I said, matter-of-factly.

I didn't have the heart to really say goodbye to him. Peonies, maybe I'd fail and Edrich was right and I'd be back, after all. Either way, I couldn't bring myself to address it.

Stephen nodded before leaning down to lift me and Maggie up into the wagon.

The wind whipped past us as he lowered us into the driver's seat. I secured Maggie, and then myself, before adjusting the series of levers and pulleys that enabled me to drive the thing to town.

"Oh," I said, pulling the letter I'd written out of my bag. "And if Uncle comes back... would you please give him this?"

He paled, but nodded, taking the sealed envelope in steady fingers and placing it in his pocket.

"May your journey be swift," he said, with a small dip of his head.

My eyes glistened, and my throat tightened a bit.

"May your troubles be few," I finally said, before signaling to Chester, my mule, that we were ready to take off. With a rocky jolt, we were on our way.

I could barely watch as the log cabin faded completely from view. Dew glistened on each blade of grass, and the soft light of the lanterns was highlighting my home, beckoning me back to it like a beacon.

I took a deep, steadying breath as Chester led us closer to town and further from the only life I'd ever known.

All I could do now was hope Edrich had changed his mind about coming with me.

✤ 6 ✤

EDRICH

I was outside the tavern well before dawn. Pepper was hunting, and Hobgoblin was happily lapping up water from a trough while I leaned against the front wall of The Poisoned Apple.

No way in hell did I want Lina out here by herself in the dead of night if she got here early. Besides, I still hoped to be able to talk her out of this.

The forest wasn't the largest one in the area, but it would still take months to explore it on foot, longer than we could possibly pack supplies for.

If we survive that long.

The peace in Neira's tavern might have been well-respected—and enforced—but very little governed the rest of Enchanted Forest. Even being human-sized and having a reasonable set of skills, the place was dangerous.

And what were the chances of us just happening to run into the tiny, hidden land of fairies? If it even existed, anymore. *If it ever has.*

"I knew you would be excited once you thought about

it!" Those were the first words she squealed when she slowed her wagon, her skin glowing a bright yellow.

Her *wagon*. That she was driving alone, the several miles it took to get here from her farm. When I had first seen it rumbling down the road in the early morning light, I had dismissed it entirely. It hadn't actually occurred to me that even Lina would be that careless.

I groaned.

"Didn't you think an unmanned wagon might attract some unwanted attention?" I pointed out.

It was hard to see in the hazy light, but I was pretty sure her skin flashed red for a second.

"It wasn't unmanned. *I* was manning it. Just like I have been for most of this year since—" She cut off, but I knew what she was going to say.

Since her mother died. I wasn't sure how I thought she'd been managing the farm since then. Mostly, I had tried not to think about any of it much, at all. I was tired of watching all the good and decent people in the world die, tired of thinking about it.

I cleared my throat.

"All right," I said, evenly. "But why take the wagon when you could have just taken the mule."

"Oh. Because I couldn't have fit all this stuff in the packs," she said brightly. "Besides, you know Maggie hates riding in the saddle bags."

"You brought your hedgehog?" My fingers went to massage the bridge of my nose.

Now I had two very small creatures to protect in a forest that was surely out to kill them. Then a flash of pink caught my eye as I noticed something else.

"Did you paint her toenails, Lina?"

"We were having a girls' night and she didn't want to be left out." She said it like it was the most obvious thing in the world.

"She told you that, did she?" I leveled a look at her.

Lina was saved from answering by the appearance of a very sleepy Vale. He ran a hand through his black hair, only managing to make it look even messier.

"Neira said you had some goods to deliver?"

"Yep, all back here." She gestured behind her before making her slow dismount from the contraption she had been sitting in.

There was a time when I would have stepped in without a thought to set her on the ground, but things weren't as easy with us, anymore. Another thing I could blame myself for, I was sure.

"Can I help, Lina?" Vale stepped forward with his palm outstretched, and she gracefully leapt onto it, her swirl of aqua-colored hair streaming behind her.

"Thank you," She beamed at him, and I felt a stab of... something.

Irritation. That was it, *of course.*

"Could you grab Maggie, too?" she asked, once she was on the ground.

I didn't know how she got so much volume for such a tiny person, but neither of us had to strain to hear her.

"Of course." He dutifully sat her hedgehog down next to her, and I noted, with some dismay, that the animal was saddled with a small pack on each side.

She really isn't joking.

That settled it. I waited until Vale had disappeared inside with one of the bundles before crouching down into a squat and speaking in a low tone.

"Lina, you can't be serious about this."

She paused with her foot halfway to the strap of the saddle, tilting her head up at me.

"Why wouldn't I be?"

"Because what if this place doesn't even exist? The forest is huge and dangerous, and this whole thing is ridiculous." I gestured to her hedgehog steed, then to the stretch of woods in the distance, that looked ominous even in the dawning light.

Maggie hissed at me, her quills around the saddle standing upright.

Lina's skin, on the other hand, turned a muted shade of blue, and I almost felt guilty before I remembered I'd rather her be sad than dead... and my father along with her. Then, it deepened to a navy color I recognized all too well, and I knew this battle was already lost.

It was determination.

"Well," she looked up at me with something like disappointment in her gaze. "Unless you believe Mama's fairy tale about my being born from a tulip, then I think it's safe to say there are other people like me out there in the world. But I suppose you would prefer that instead of finding them, I stay here, in a world that wasn't built for me, on a farm where I have no one left?" *Is that last part accusatory, or is it only my remorse making it seem that way?*

I swallowed, looking around at the world through her eyes for a change. The horse's hoof that was nearly as tall as she was. The wagon that had to be modified just for her to steer it.

Then I thought about the farm without her on it, and I realized maybe my motives for trying to keep her here weren't as pure as keeping her safe, or even keeping my father safe. But that didn't mean I was wrong.

"*If* they exist, that doesn't change the fact that we don't even know where we're going, Lina."

"They *do* exist. I came from somewhere. And I do know where we're going." She wouldn't quite meet my eyes. "I have a map." Her skin flickered a bit as she pulled out a small bit of parchment.

She was lying, but not about the map, so... "You don't know where we're going, do you?"

She looked off to the side. "I practically do."

I opened my mouth to argue, but she cut me off.

"If you think this is so stupid, why did you even come?"

"To talk you out of it," I shot back.

But she didn't turn pale blue, or even the crimson shade of anger. Her color was still resolutely navy when she smiled up at me, gesturing to my back.

"Then why did you pack?"

She had me there. Rising to my feet, I shook my head as I muttered down at her, "Have you ever tried to talk you out of anything?"

7

LINA

I wasn't sure if I should take Edrich's statement as a compliment or an insult, so I settled on the former, and nodded to myself.

Is it so bad to be persuasive? Besides... What do I have to lose at this point?

I shook my head and squared my shoulders.

"Listen, Edrich. I know you have a busy life, and you probably are needed somewhere else... " I felt my resolve harden. If I had to do this alone, so be it. "So you don't have to go, if you don't want to," I added, hesitantly. "But I do."

I patted Maggie on the head and secured her saddle-bags once more, just to give my hands something to do.

Vale came back out with a dolly to load several more parcels from the wagon. He made quick work of it, looking between Edrich and me like he could physically see the tension there, before silently steering the packages through the tavern doors.

Edrich didn't respond. His shoulders were tense, and

the little crinkle between his brows was deeper than normal. When his lips parted, I expected him to disappoint me, but instead the next sound I heard was that of a bird crying out as a shadow appeared over my head.

The shadow grew larger and larger as I stared up at a stunning flash of black and white. My mouth fell open as the shape gained speed, flying closer and closer until Edrich yelled.

"No!" He said the word like an order, stepping between me and Maggie and the rapidly descending bird.

Maggie curled up into a ball, her spikes standing on end, while I peeked around the side of his boot.

The bird flew back up toward the sky, making a circle, before deciding to land on his arm. Its wings continued to flap, sending gusts of wind down on my head, making it hard to keep my balance.

Edrich used the straps of leather attached to the bird's legs to tether it to his arm.

"She's... she's beautiful!" I stammered, taking in each stunning, white feather, peppered with small black vees.

"She almost ate you!" He growled.

I stopped studying the bird for a moment to gawk at him.

"What? No, I don't believe that. She wants to be friends." I smiled up at the creature, completely in awe of her. "Spiders are the only ones who can't be trusted. Most birds, however, can be won over, eventually."

Magnolia, however, felt very differently. She practically rolled away, hiding behind the wheel of Chester's wagon.

Edrich groaned and placed a small hood over the bird's head.

"That's your problem, Lina. You think everyone and

everything is as nice as you are." He threw his head back as the sound of Maggie snorting in protest came from behind me.

"That's not true." I shot him a half smile. "I never think you're nice."

He let out a short burst of air, one I would have called a laugh from someone else.

"As for Pepper, she just wanted to meet me." I quirked an eyebrow and placed my hands on my hips as I studied the two of them. "And since when do you have *pets*?" I used the word he hated so much.

Pets shouldn't be a thing, according to him. He had always had a soft spot for animals. Even as a kid, he would take them in, bandaging them, stitching them up, helping them when he could. He was even the reason that I'd met Maggie. But he'd never kept one before.

"She's not a— You know what, it doesn't matter. I don't know why I bother trying to argue with you when I'd have better luck with the mule."

I shrugged, because I didn't know why either.

"You worry too much. We'll all be fast friends, you'll see." I beamed up at them.

The ringing of bells alerted us that Vale had opened the door again. He silently glanced back and forth between Edrich and me for a moment before speaking.

"Are you going to be all right, Lina?" He ran his fingers through his thick, black waves. "You know I'd be willing to come with you, if you needed a friend."

I couldn't help but glow a little at his offer. Smiling, I opened my mouth to respond, but was cut off by an annoyed Edrich.

"She'll be fine. She has all the company she needs."

An uncomfortable look crossed Vale's features before he looked back down at me.

"Lina?" Ignoring Edrich, Vale crouched so he was only a few feet taller than me, instead of the usual six.

"I'll be fine, Vale," I said, moving closer so I could squeeze his hand.

He took a deep breath, as if he was trying to decide whether or not I meant it.

"Vale, I promise. But thank you," I assured him.

"If you insist," he said, pressing his lips together in a tight line. He gently brushed a fingertip along my cheek, and I leaned into his touch.

I didn't miss the way Edrich shifted uncomfortably behind me.

"Well, at least take these for the journey." Vale handed me a small package—small enough to fit into Maggie's bags—before reluctantly handing Edrich a larger one.

The smell of cookies and warm bread permeated the air around me, and I was practically drooling as I packed mine away.

"Thank you for always being so thoughtful." I smiled up at him.

Vale inclined his head toward me before standing and giving Edrich an awkward goodbye.

He promised to return Chester to the farm, and even to check in on Stephen and the Adlers while I was away. The hesitant smile he sent my way before closing the doors to The Poisoned Apple behind him was enough to bolster my confidence. If Vale wasn't trying to talk me out of this, then he believed in me. *That was all the encouragement I needed.*

Edrich pointedly cleared his throat behind me, and I spun around.

"So, does this mean you're coming with me?" I grinned, wildly.

He gave a long suffering sigh. "Looks that way."

"You won't regret it," I said, though it wasn't a promise I should've made. Then, coaxing Magnolia out of her ball, I beckoned her to me. "Come on, girl. It's time to go."

Climbing onto Maggie's saddle, I set off toward the forest with Edrich and Pepper at my side.

8

EDRICH

Enchanted Forest was a pretty name for people who saw interesting, beautiful things and thought they were magical... people who never had to look long enough to see that those things were more likely to kill you than to "enchant" you.

At least it wasn't raining like yesterday, though the humidity hinted that it might soon. Still, it was cool enough to justify my long sleeved shirt, especially once we got into the shade of the forest.

We neared the entrance, and a chill crept down my spine that had nothing to do with the cooler temperatures. It was a familiar feeling from years of hunting, like there was a predator nearby.

We passed several signs warning in multiple languages and hieroglyphics to turn back, which did nothing to curb the waterfall of dread pooling in my stomach.

Any hope of Lina aborting this plan of hers went out the window with one look at her unwavering navy skin.

There was no way in a dwarven mine that she was going to change her mind.

The Enchanted Forest spread out before us like an unwelcoming expanse. The sun seemed to disappear in the forest itself, shying away from the path as if it, too, was too afraid to enter.

Lina didn't bother to wait for me as she and Maggie strode forward, her body rocking from the movement of her hedgehog. She didn't turn around to see if I would follow, either, but I did.

What choice do I have?

The tall, wide-trunked trees had only a narrow pathway through them for the entrance.

Lina and I weren't conversing, but I wouldn't go so far as to say we passed the time in silence. She hummed while she looked at her map and chattered away at Maggie, singing under her breath when she got distracted. She was constant motion and sound and more *life* than it felt like I had seen in ages.

Although, in a place where being still and silent would keep you alive, it was hard to appreciate her vivacity just then.

As much as the sun didn't want to shine through the forest, I was surprised by the glowing moss on many of the trees. They lit our path like small lanterns with enough light that Lina seemed to have no trouble reading the small, hand-drawn map she was holding.

"So, tell me about this map of yours," I said, mostly to interrupt her latest line of cooing at the hedgehog.

Even if she hadn't been intentionally hiding it, I would have had a hard time making out the tiny markings on the square inch of parchment. *What does she even use to write with?* I had never asked her, and it brought her comment earlier uncomfortably back to mind.

This world really wasn't built for her. I had never thought she minded that before, but maybe that was just one more way I had managed to kid myself back then.

"It's more of a concept map," she finally said, "based on a few things I've managed to pick up. But the general direction is—" She looked around at the sun peeking through the leaves and the tree line, before pointing toward the northwest. "Somewhere in there."

She sounded so proud of herself that even I couldn't bring myself to tell her that "somewhere in there" was still a whole lot of ground to search for a kingdom that could probably fit in the wagon she had ridden in.

"All right," I said, instead. "That way, it is."

We walked for a few more minutes in relative silence, aside from the occasional disgruntled noises Pepper made from her spot at my shoulder, still no happier with Lina's presence than she was before.

Which, frankly, made two of us. Especially as a neon-blue frog jumped from the underbrush and made it halfway to Lina before I kicked it away. Not that she seemed to notice. The poisonous frog hadn't even interrupted her humming.

Her color, though, was slightly off, and it occurred to me that she might be humming to distract herself as much as anything.

"Lina's lucky to have you looking out for her."

Those were some of the last words her mother had spoken to me before I had abruptly left the small village we called home. It hadn't been true then, and it sure as hell didn't feel true now, but it did make me feel guilty enough to at least try to talk to her.

"So... how have you been, since... " I trailed off, uncomfortably.

"It's all right, Edrich." There was wry amusement in her tone. "You can say, since she died. And... I'm fine."

That wasn't an answer to what I had actually asked, but I wasn't going to push her to talk about her feelings.

"And you?" she asked.

"Same old, same old." Same job that wasn't, at all, what I thought it would be when Atesh had approached me about my falconry skills nearly three years ago, now.

My family had been struggling, and he said his band always had extra work. He said it casually, like they were a regular band of mercenaries, not the Huntsmen, the most elite, sought-after mercenaries this side of the world.

I kicked away an enormous rat creature halfway to a still oblivious Lina, my thoughts still lingering in the past.

Besides, the pay was more than my mother made in a year with her sewing jobs, and the cause seemed noble enough. I suppose it was, at the time.

Later, though...

"The girl at the bar?"

I belatedly realized Lina was asking me a question.

"What?" I asked.

"I was just wondering if you had a... girl, somewhere." Her voice was a little quieter than it had been. "If that's why you never come home."

I stopped in my tracks, staring down at her.

"You think I missed your mother's funeral for a girl?"

Though actually, that reason was better than the real one —better than her knowing I had been busy making a deal for the freedom of the Huntsmen that would wind up costing all of our souls. *Maybe I should have let it slide.*

"I just wondered." She shrugged casually, but her skin was deep pink.

"No, Lina." I started walking again, swatting buzzing insects out of my way before they could make their way down to her. "There's no girl."

"Then who was—"

She was cut off as a rhino beetle, at least half as tall as she was, emerged from a blanket of leaves. Its mottled-green color had blended with the forest floor until it was inches from her.

Cursing, I brought my boot down on it.

"What did you do that for?" Lina gasped. "Maybe it was just saying hello."

"With its pincers?" I shot back.

"Maybe." She lifted her chin defiantly, and I just shook my head.

This forest was already living up to its reputation, and we were only a few hundred yards in. We needed a better plan.

"I think it would be better if I carried you. Both of you," I reluctantly amended, looking at Maggie. *This trek just gets better and better.*

"We're fine down here," Lina said sunnily, though it sounded a little forced.

I examined her for a moment, the way she was holding herself a little too stiffly. *Is she scared and just too stubborn to admit it? Or is it something else?*

"You really aren't," I said back.

Though, I could see why she thought so since she kept conveniently misinterpreting the intention of every creature we came across.

"Honestly, Edrich." She sat up straighter. "I don't know what you're so worried about. I'm *from* this forest."

I suppressed a groan, trying not to draw any more unwanted attention. "No, Lina. Your people might be from here, and they might not, but *you* are from the middle of apple-picking nowhere, the same as me!"

Her mouth formed an offended *O*, and she let out a squeak of indignation as I picked her up with one hand, and Maggie with the other. The blasted hedgehog hissed and raised her quills, stabbing my hand.

I cursed and nearly dropped her as Lina tried to comfort the thing. Pepper snapped at them, and I shooed her away, grinding my teeth in frustration.

There has to be a way to make this work.

I mentally tallied my inventory. There was a way... but Lina was not going to like it.

"If Maggie rides in the pouch of my pack," I told her, "you can ride in my front pocket."

Sure enough, her bare arms turned a deep crimson.

"You want me to ride... in your pocket?" She didn't sound nearly as sunny anymore.

"*Want* is a strong word," I said, evenly. "But it seems like the best option."

"There has to be a less humiliating option... "

"It's the option that's least likely to get you killed." I narrowed my eyes at her, trying to figure out why she was being so uncharacteristically difficult.

"Fine. Great. Just put me in your pocket, then, like a bit of spare change."

"Lina—" I started, but she cut me off.

"No, it's fine." She grimaced and reached for my pocket, then refused to say another word.

❧ 9 ❧

LINA

Pain lanced through my back, and I was secretly grateful—in spite of my initial argument—that I had the privacy of Edrich's shirt pocket to hide in. It was excruciating. A kind of searing agony burning up and down my spine and shoulder blades.

The thick, soft fabric of his shirt concealed the pulsating colors ebbing off of me. Every inch of me hurt, and my ointment, or what was left of it, was in Maggie's saddle bag.

I took slow, measured breaths and tried to wait out the aching. This spasm seemed to last longer than the others. I only had a few days' supply left, if that. I told myself that was why I didn't ask Edrich to hand it to me. *Or why I wouldn't mention I was even in pain, at all.*

Perhaps I'd need it more later on...

I couldn't wrap my head around why I was having so many flare-ups lately.

Is it because I can't reach my entire back? Am I not using it enough?

I distracted myself by inhaling the heady smell of campfire and meadows that radiated off of him. Then there was the freshly baked chocolate cookie from Vale nestled next to me. The combination smelled like home, and it was easy to imagine myself somewhere else for a moment.

I eyed the cookie again. *At least I can seek solace for my stomach, if not for anything else.*

When the pain finally subsided, I slowly stood to peer out of Edrich's pocket. He hadn't said anything in ages. Not since he saw that I was lying to him.

I hated the distance that had grown between us over the years. I'd tried to pretend I hadn't noticed. I'd tried to make everything normal.

But I'd felt it, deep in my bones. Maybe bringing him with me was a last-ditch effort at maintaining a friendship that had dissolved long ago... ending it on a better note than it had been over the past several years.

I felt, more than saw, myself turning a pale shade of blue.

No.

I couldn't believe that. Friendships made in youth are cemented for life... right?

I shook off the different sort of ache that thought filled me with, and stood at my full height, resting my arms on the rim of Edrich's pocket. I only looked up at him when I was certain I was my normal coloring again.

He was focused on the path before us. From this vantage point, the forest looked a little less daunting.

The trees still towered over us, the trunks wider than any back on the farm. And the bark was so dark, it was almost black. Leaves of every shade of green and blue and yellow and red hung heavy on the branches as Edrich ducked between their grasps. If I didn't know any better, I'd swear it was almost as if they had fingers and were trying to hold onto us in an attempt to keep us here forever.

So maybe not that much less daunting, then. I gulped.

You are not afraid, Lina. This is probably, most definitely, your home... so there is no reason to be afraid. Probably...

I repeated the words silently to myself as twigs snapped under Edrich's feet and eerie sounds came from deep in the woods ahead of us.

This is your true home. You belong here.

The more I assured myself of these things, the more I believed it.

Soon, the eerie sounds coming from somewhere in the distance began to sound more like a melody. The crickets played a rhythm matched by the rustling of branches and shaking of leaves. Even the growling of a creature in time with its own stomping began to lend itself as bass to the song the forest sang.

As I relaxed, Edrich only seemed to become more rigid. The crease between his brow furrowed and deepened as he lost himself in whatever thoughts were plaguing him.

"I can feel you staring." His deep voice practically reverberated against me in his pocket.

"You sure you know where you're going?" I finally asked with a smile and a quirk of my eyebrow, trying to soften his demeanor.

He peered down at me, his countenance beginning to mirror my own.

Only, instead of the boy I'd known all of my life

looking back at me, it was a man I only barely recognized. The beginning of a beard was forming on his face, and the circles under his thick lashes were a dark blue. His once soft expression was hardened and haunted. The thick, blond waves that used to cascade over his brow, were now tightly pulled back into a knot behind his head.

It wasn't until I saw the corner of his mouth twitch that I realized he was going to let our earlier conversation go. When his lips eventually stretched into a reluctant smile, relief washed through me. He rolled his eyes and sighed.

"Maybe if I could read that sorry excuse for a map you have, I would know for sure." He answered my earlier question. Then he glanced back at his pocket and shook his head. "Did you really just decide to help yourself to my cookie?"

I returned his grin and wiped away whatever evidence still lingered on my face.

"First of all, it's your fault for putting me in here with the temptation and for not ever breaking for lunch. But also, that map wasn't made for *you,*" I said, sticking out my tongue, earning a reluctant chuckle. "But I would be happy to guide you, oh Surly One."

This time his laugh was heartier, the sound rich and deep.

"All right, *Thumbelina*." He emphasized the old nickname he'd given me. "Lead the way."

10

EDRICH

I had forgotten how impossible it was to stay irritated with Lina.

It was easier to resent her when we were apart, but not when I looked at her smirking face and knew she had no idea of the way her existence had shackled my life. *It's not her fault I bound myself to protect her.* It was mine, and Rumplestiltskin's.

And that wasn't why I hated to be around her, not really. I knew that, even if it was hard to admit it most of the time.

Every hint of anger slowly drained away, but not the tension—not when we were intruding on the homes of a thousand creatures that would try to kill both of us, and not when she was staring at me like that. Like I was some knight in shining armor instead of just a mercenary.

We made steady progress following the basic direction of her map, but it wasn't without detours. Pepper scouted constantly ahead. When she cawed out a warning, we knew to give the area in front of us a wide berth.

Even with my falcon, we had a few near-misses. Too many, considering we were still on the relative outskirts of the forest. I was so lost in my thoughts and my constant perusal of the forest, it took me a while to figure out why it was getting chillier and harder to see. Night was falling.

"We should find a stopping point," I told Lina.

"Oh, I guess we should." She glanced around, sounding dubious, so I raised my eyebrows in question.

"I usually just find a nice enclosed flower if I'm away from home." She shrugged.

I couldn't help the laugh that escaped my lips. *Of course, she does.*

"Well, as much as I would love to just curl up in a tulip for the night, I'll have to set some shelter up somewhere, hopefully out of the way."

"Would you?" She tilted her head in question.

"Would I what?"

"Love to be small enough to curl up in a flower and sleep?"

I would have laughed the question off, but she was peering up at my face like she was searching for something... like the answer mattered.

Visions flitted through my mind, the difficulties of being small. But... not everything I envisioned was bad. Something else occurred to me also, something I didn't want to delve too deeply into.

"I guess I don't know," I finally said. It was as close to the truth as either of us were getting tonight.

She didn't say anything after that, just kept shooting questioning looks my way.

I was grateful when I found a relatively flat, hidden

space under a low-hanging branch to hang a makeshift tent. It was the work of a few seconds to unroll the water-proof canvas from my bag and secure it in place, and the varied coloring should be enough to keep us somewhat hidden, at least from predators that hunted with their eyes.

We couldn't do much to cover up our scents, but we had known that coming into this. At least, I had.

I turned at the sound of clinking to see random things being pushed outside of my bag.

"What all do you have in here?" Lina's voice echoed from inside the canvas. Upon closer inspection, I saw a greenish glow coming from the bag as well.

"Dare I even ask what you're doing?"

"Maggie and I are just exploring," she called back. "Along with our helpful friend."

A low, reluctant chuckle escaped my lips while I opened the bag to find a glowing snail lighting the way for Lina while she systematically sorted through my carefully packed things. Though, she probably could have lit the way herself, the way she was still glowing with each heartbeat.

"What's in the flask?" she asked, curiously.

"Bourbon. Are you finished?"

"Not when you've been withholding the good stuff," she called back.

"Says the woman who ate my cookie," I reminded her.

She rummaged around for a few more minutes, reminding me how strong she was for such a tiny person. She picked up my heavy flask and the solid knife with ease, setting them to the side. When she made her way to my underclothes, I reached in and plucked her out, following up to remove the snail and a more amenable Maggie, as well.

"Okay, you're done here."

She didn't argue, just announced it was time to change her clothes. Only she would insist on wearing pajamas to sleep in the middle of the Enchanted Forest, but there was exactly zero point in arguing with her.

I heard a few hisses and grunts, then she muttered one of her ridiculous curse words under her breath.

"Lina, why are you in pain?" I called over my shoulder.

Instead of answering, she just hitched in another breath.

"Lina?"

"It's nothing," she finally breathed out.

"It's obviously something," I pushed back.

There was another beat of silence before she mumbled.

"It's umm... it's cramps, okay?"

"Oh. Sorry." My face heated, and I was glad she couldn't see. "Sorry," I said again, casting around for a way to steer the subject away from my invasive line of questioning.

"Aren't you going to change?" She saved me the trouble of coming up with something to say.

"No. I'll just sleep in this." Despite my thoughts about her pajamas, I had to admit one of us had been more prepared than the other for the possibility of sleeping in close quarters. When I traveled with the men, we just took our clothes off to sleep, and put them back on in the morning, but that obviously wouldn't work here. I hadn't thought about it, really.

With a resigned sigh, I climbed into my bedroll fully-dressed. I could at least spare us that one small bit of awkwardness.

For once.

11

LINA

The forest was loud. Even within the confines of the tent Edrich had pitched, the bugs and trees and animals echoed all around us, continuing their melody from earlier in the day at a higher volume.

Or maybe it was the fact that we'd been sitting silently next to the small fire he had made. *Small for him, but easily a bonfire to me.*

Edrich plucked the last few savory mushrooms off of the stick he'd used to roast them, placing them on a thick green leaf and sprinkling them with a small vial of salt from his satchel.

I applauded the feast he set out for us; berries, roasted mushrooms, and a few dried figs.

"It's perfect!" I squealed, diving in and devouring the small pieces he'd cut up for me.

"Hardly. But it will do, I suppose." Edrich ate his portion before lying down on his bedroll with a sigh.

I ate my fill and made sure to share with Maggie to

supplement the mealworms she'd dug up. As I savored the last morsel, a thought struck me.

"Oh no! Shouldn't we have saved some for Pepper?" I darted a glance outside of the tent, but Edrich laughed.

"Pepper likes her food... a bit more rare than we do."

I gulped, my skin alternating between shades of pale green and pearl.

"Right. How silly of me. But, will she be all right out there on her own?" We hadn't heard her caw in hours and I was beginning to worry. "Will she know where to find us?"

"She knows. She's used to this sort of thing. Usually when I'm out with Atesh or the other hunts—*soldiers,* she scouts ahead and comes back when she's ready."

Just as I was about to respond, Edrich yawned and declared that he was tired.

The statement felt abrupt, but then again, it was rather late and he had to do all of the walking for us. So, I nodded and laid out my own bedroll next to the small fire.

Maggie curled up next to me in a small pile of leaves, snuggling the scrap of blanket I'd brought for her, and it wasn't long before the gentle rhythm of her snores began.

I tried to make myself comfortable on the thin bedding, but my back was still tight, and my blankets smelled like the farmhouse, like home... somehow, that made me both happy and sad at the same time.

Will I ever go back?

The thought came crashing in, just as another spasm decided to rack my spine.

Tears pricked at my eyes, but I squeezed them tight against the pain, doing my best to breathe through it.

I crawled to Maggie's saddle and fumbled around the bag for my ointment, nearly falling over in the process. I was striving so hard for silence. If Edrich was sleeping, I didn't want to wake him, not for this. A nearly silent gasp escaped my lips from the ache of twisting my arm behind me. I stretched as much as I could to apply what little was left of the ointment to whatever area I could reach.

Another deep breath and slow exhale.

Magnolia stirred beside me, sneezing as soon as the bitter scent of the medicine reached her. Her eyes shot open, and she inched closer, nuzzling my arm, providing whatever comfort she could. She was used to seeing the spasms. Especially as they'd increased their frequency since Mama...

I trailed off at the thought. One kind of intense pain was all I could manage at a time.

Another slow, ragged breath, and I was through the worst of it.

"You, uh, all right?" Edrich's voice sounded, and I stiffened. "You know, with your... cramps?"

He could barely form the word, and his awkwardness was nearly laughable.

His inability to stomach talk of "female woes" had not gotten better with age.

Maybe I was wrong for lying to him, but he had enough to worry about with his constant fretting over whether I'd be eaten by a beetle, let alone if he knew I was in pain. He'd never take me through the Enchanted Forest if he thought I was sick or having flare-ups again.

He'd seen them a few times when we were younger, but as far as he knew, I'd outgrown them. Sadly, I hadn't. The excruciating pain was just a part of my life and I had grown tired of being the poor, small, suffering girl who was completely helpless. I wanted to help others, not be constantly pitied for everything about myself...

"I'm better now," I responded, with a tight smile. "Thank you."

His hand came up to smooth out the tight knot in his hair.

"You, uh, sure?" He coughed, unable to look directly at me. "Do you... need anything?"

He glanced over me, and around me, and at the tent above us—anywhere but at me. This time, I couldn't help but laugh.

"You're blushing. You're actually blushing!" I teased.

The red in his cheeks deepened, and I laughed again.

Edrich rolled his eyes and turned over on his blanket. Like a child. The mirth continued to roll out of me until finally, reluctantly, he chuckled, too. I could swear I even heard Pepper cawing with laughter somewhere off in the distance.

"It's nice to know you're feeling well enough to make fun of me, you imp."

I feigned offense as he turned back around to study me, but I couldn't keep the pretense for long.

"Yes, I'm feeling much better now," I said, grinning and wiping away tears from my eyes. "Much, much better."

"Har. Har," he added drily. But I saw the whisper of a smile tempting his lips.

I fell asleep, peacefully, for the first time in ages with that image in my mind.

12

EDRICH

"**N**o!" *The woman's scream echoed over and over again. "Don't take my babies to her! I'll do anything."*

Even knowing this was a dream, I had no more power to change the outcome than I had that day.

Dream Atesh looked at me with the same expression he had held then, one I still couldn't decipher. Had he been thinking the same thing I was? Was it worth our lives to go back on our word for this mission?

The penalty, by law, for any mercenary defecting was death, even if the queen's men didn't find us first. Her reach seemed to have no limits. I pictured Lina's farmhouse and the cottage where I had grown up set ablaze, everyone I'd ever loved still trapped inside as the flames shattered the windows and engulfed the doors.

The queen had done worse to those who betrayed her.

We should have known when she came into the dungeon offering us freedom in exchange for a "small favor." But we had been desperate, all six of us imprisoned for reasons no one had explained.

Of course, it made sense now. Atesh had told her no once

before. None of us wanted to work for a queen who was known to brutalize anyone who got in her way.

What did the horrible woman even want with a family, anyway, except to extend her particular brand of destruction into every bit of happiness she found?

The littlest child sobbed and clung to her mother's skirts, but the older boy didn't take his eyes off me.

"Are you proud of yourself?" His words resounded in my dream, on repeat.

No, I wanted to tell him. And I never will be again.

I had taken part in this. Pepper and I had found them. Then we'd gone with the Huntsmen to deliver them across the border into Floriend where black-armored soldiers threw the defenseless woman, her knocked-out husband, and all three children into the back of a jailer's wagon. All the while, the boy's eyes bored into mine. I didn't drop his gaze, though. Even in my shame, I knew he deserved that much. It might be the last bit of respect anyone paid to him.

Because there sure as hell wouldn't be any once the queen got a hold of them.

"Edrich?" Atesh was trying to break me out of the spell I was under, watching the wagon grow fainter in the distance.

"Edrich?" He said it again, but this time, his voice sounded more feminine, and distinctly more urgent.

"Edrich!"

I jolted awake at the sound of a woman's frantic whisper. It took me a moment to remember where I was and who was speaking. It was Lina. We were in a tent, in the forest. *Why did she sound so urgent?*

It was too dark to make out her features.

"What's wrong?" I whispered.

"I think... I think there's something outside the tent," she spoke quietly, right into my ear.

Sitting up, I rubbed the sweat from my brow and bit back a sigh. There were probably lots of *somethings* outside the tent. We were, after all, in the middle of the forest where countless creatures lived. Still, I strained my ears for a moment and cursed internally.

There was definitely someone—or something—out there. *Something big.*

Not a leaf crackled or a branch crunched. It was more the absence of sound than the presence of it that unnerved me. The cut-off squeal of a smaller creature, the muted pad of a very large footstep.

I didn't want to risk more noise by telling Lina to be quiet, but for once, she seemed content to make no noise all on her own. Only her barely audible breaths told me she was still next to me at all.

Mentally, I reviewed our options. I had a knife and a sword, but there was no telling how big the thing was or if there was more than one of them. It hadn't attacked yet, so that was something. The smartest thing to do would be to stay here and hope we avoided notice.

No sooner had the thought crossed my mind than a grunt sounded directly outside the tent, and the top of the canvas strained like something was pressing against it.

Son of a goblin.

A massive snout sniffed at the edge of the canvas. The hot, heavy air that the beast huffed out filled our small space, practically gagging both of us with the smell of rancid breath. It reeked of death and decay, and a shiver ran down my spine.

This wasn't a normal bear or wolf, both of which I'd

encountered before. This was something bigger, and, I suspected, far deadlier.

The slow ripping of fabric sounded as long, glowing spines began to tear through our shelter.

Sweet fairy hell. I'm going to have to fight this thing—or run. The latter might be the better option with Lina to consider, as well.

Blood rushed to my temples, and I secured Lina in my breast pocket and Maggie in my satchel for the quick getaway we were about to make. I bit back a curse as the hedgehog bristled and bit my finger hard for having woken her up.

Slowly, silently, I raised myself into a sprinting position, ready to run us far away from whatever was out there. My hand gripped the hilt of the sword next to me. Just as I was about to rip open the slit of the carefully draped tent, Pepper cawed loudly overhead.

The heavy breathing cut off abruptly, then the sound of soft footfalls receded.

Pepper's distraction must have been enough for the creature, or creatures, to decide they weren't interested in us.

It was another solid ten minutes before I even dared to let loose a sigh of relief. Gently, I sat Lina back down onto the ground. Again, I didn't have to tell her to remain silent. In fact, only minutes later, the sound of her even, peaceful breaths filled the tent.

At least one of us will get some sleep tonight.

I WAS RIGHT ABOUT NOT GETTING any sleep. After the near miss with whatever that thing was, I woke at every snapping twig, or even when there was a stretch of silence too long.

Finally, when there was the slightest shaft of light to see by, I got up to dismantle the tent. Lina slept through me reorganizing my pack and rolling up the canvas to our tent, even through Maggie's grunting as she pulled a few worms from the ground less than a foot away from Lina's head. She didn't stir at all until I gently tapped the ground next to her.

She bolted upright.

"Peonies!" She looked up at me. "Oh, it's just you. I thought there was an earthquake for a second."

I guess I didn't tap so gently, after all.

"Sorry, it's time to go," I said. "That is, if you still want to go forward." I was hoping last night had put the danger into perspective for her.

"Of course, I do," she said, way too brightly for someone who had only been awake about three seconds. "Why wouldn't I?"

She yawned and stretched her arms wide, perfectly content, as if she had entirely forgotten what transpired last night.

"Oh, I don't know. Because something came very close to making us its dinner?" I said.

"It was just curious." She waved a hand dismissively.

"Sure it was. Giant predators are always 'just curious' about smaller edible things." I pointed out the enormous paw-prints in the soft earth around the tent, easily twice the size of my hand. Lina could have taken one of her cozy naps in the indentation of the thing's pinky toe.

"Then why didn't it eat us?" She smiled up at me like she had won the argument.

Well, she might have been chipper this early in the morning, but that only made one of us. I let out a frustrated growl.

"I'm serious, Lina. Have you considered that finding this tiny world won't do you much good if you're dead?"

Finally, her skin faded from the bright rose-gold to something more muted, and some immature part of me was glad to see her show some reasonable reaction.

"Have you considered," she asked, quietly, "that being alive won't do me much good with the kind of life I have now?"

Whatever response I had been crafting died on my lips. Suddenly, there was no part of me that was happy to have gotten a reaction from her.

"You can't mean that," I said, kneeling down to be closer to her.

She got to her feet, bridging the gap between us by another inch.

"I don't know, Edrich." She shook her head sadly, her color turning the palest blue, looking even more muted against her bright yellow nightgown. "What is there in my life back there? Trying to keep the farm running, alone?"

"You're not—" I started to argue with her, but she cut me off.

"How could you possibly know that when you're never around?" She shot me an incredulous look, but didn't wait for my response before she continued. "Yes, I am alone. And I will always be alone, as long as I stay there. You— you can get married." Her voice broke on that word. "You can have a family. You can get a *hug* from your friends."

Tears slipped down her cheeks, and she stared at the ground. "It's not about the everyday mechanics of getting around, as frustrating as those can be. It's about my life. It's about my *future*."

Had she always been this miserable, and I had just been too blind to see it? It stung in an unexpected way I couldn't quite explain to myself. I could hardly argue if that was how she felt, though, so I said nothing.

That seems to be my specialty, after all.

13

LINA

I t had been hours since we spoke. Edrich's jaw twitched on and off, and his breathing hitched a few times, as if he wanted to say something, but thought better of it.

Perhaps it's better this way.

Edrich made us a small breakfast while I hid behind a large, purple mushroom to change. Once I was in a simple cotton tunic with hand-stitched roses embroidered on the hem and matching trousers, I folded up my blankets and nightgown, nestling them back into my pack. Edrich had taken no time at all to pack his gear. It was an efficiency one could only expect from a soldier who was used to traveling.

Few words were communicated before breakfast was finished and he picked me up, but allowed Maggie to travel on the ground this time. I asked why she got to walk when I couldn't, and his response was pointed.

"Because she can walk and run faster than you. And she's covered in spikes. Do you have spikes?" The matter-of-fact tone he used was almost worse than if he had been intentionally mean.

I bit back a childish response about his own spiky demeanor and kept silent, instead. Checking my map, and his compass, I gave him some basic directions, and then we were off.

My skin tingled with agitation, and sitting in his pocket wasn't helping the feeling to subside. His heartbeat raced beneath the fabric of his shirt. His skin may not have given away his feelings like mine did, but he had his own tells.

Rubbing my face, I stifled a groan. I needed to pace; to walk, to run, to be doing anything but stay still and allow this feeling to build. Our conversation played on a loop in my mind, my last statement ringing out louder than the rest.

How long have I felt this way?

My words to Edrich rang too true as I spoke them. It was something that had crossed my mind from time to time, but I'd never lent much weight to it until this morning. Until I'd spoken it into the air, making it somehow truer than before.

I wasn't in the practice of wanting or longing for things I couldn't have. *What was the point in that?* While Mama was alive, I'd been happy—content even—with the life she'd built us. With her gone, what was left was an emptiness that had likely been there all along in some small part of my heart. Something I hadn't noticed or allowed myself to focus on before.

I was somewhere between being proud of myself for being so blunt with Edrich, and regretting every word that put this ogre-sized issue between us again. There was no taking the words back, though. I'd said them, and I'd meant them... even if I wished I hadn't.

We continued heading northwest, according to Edrich's compass, stopping only a few times for him to rest his legs and for me to stretch and check on Maggie.

My hedgehog had been delightedly following close by, happy with the freedom to snack on bugs and berries she found along the path. This forest called to her the same way it called to me. I could sense it.

The third place we stopped was my favorite. The air was sweeter, ripe with the scent of summer's end. Colorful fruit hung from the trees and bushes around us, animals tittered and scurried nearby, completely unbothered by our presence. There was a stream with dancing lilies on top of the water. Butterflies and bumblebees flitted from each of the flowers, and back again.

Wild mushrooms grew on the bark of trees in shapes and sizes I'd never dreamed of before. Some looked like spun sugar, white and frosty and fine. Some were dense and glowing and every shade of the rainbow. And still more had spots and designs that looked as if they'd been hand-painted.

Lifting my arms, I spun around, allowing the gentle breeze to whip through my hair and the fringes of my dress, making me feel lighter than I had all day.

Making me feel like I can fly.

Maggie sniffed at the air before her eyes locked on to something in the distance. Suddenly, she was nothing more than a ball of spikes, rolling under the bushes nearby.

A shadow grew overhead, and Pepper's caw rang out. Edrich's eyes went wide with fear as she swooped down and landed next to me. She was fast, faster than any bird

I'd ever seen. And far faster than Edrich as he desperately tried to bridge the meter between us to get to me.

"Lina!"

"Edrich, it's fine," I said, reaching out toward her.

Before Edrich could reach us, I was petting her, and she was pressing her head into my touch.

I couldn't help the giggle that escaped me when she practically burrowed her beak under my arm, in an effort to get as close as she possibly could. She let out a few soft chirps each time I stroked her feathers.

Edrich's jaw was practically on the ground.

14

EDRICH

I rolled my eyes at the cooing sounds Lina was making to my deadly gyrfalcon. We had been back on our trek for a solid half hour, with Lina securely in my pocket and Pepper on my shoulder, and her attention hadn't faltered. Worse still, Pepper was eating them up, like she was one of Lina's furry woodland friends, instead of a fierce bird of prey.

I had forgotten the way Lina always seemed to do that, in the end. Once I had found her caught in a spider web, merrily chattering away at an enormous wolf spider who actually appeared to be listening to her.

Or, at least not eating her, which was something.

It wasn't the only thing I had forgotten, either. Or, more accurately, tried not to think about. When I was gone, it was easy to forget the way she had this unyielding faith in me, as though she thought there was nothing I couldn't do.

I hated the way it almost made me hope I was everything she thought I was, instead of the person I had actually become.

"Why are you so angry?" Lina's question startled me from my thoughts.

"I'm not," I lied, automatically.

"Yes, you are," she said simply. "I can feel your heart thundering with it, even if I can't see your face."

"*Can* you see my face from that angle?" I tried to change the subject, carefully picking my way around several holes in the ground that looked like they might house small, ground-dwelling creatures.

Probably venomous ones, given our luck.

"Yes, Edrich." She sounded as exasperated as I'd ever heard her. "I can. You didn't answer my question."

And I wasn't going to. She wouldn't begin to understand that I was still angry from visceral memories of being held in a dank cell for something I hadn't done. Of watching my brothers be dragged away to have information "extracted" from them. Of dragging an innocent family to the same woman who had tortured us.

I focused on the small relief of having safely reached the other side of the holes, but Lina needled again.

"Edrich?"

I narrowed my eyes at her, but her resolutely navy skin and the stubborn tilt of her chin told me I was getting nowhere. I scowled.

Pepper flitted irritably on my shoulder until I prodded her to take flight again, but the silence she left in her wake wasn't much better. The light footsteps I was forced to use did nothing to give my anger an outlet, either.

Another couple minutes of Lina tapping her foot in my pocket is what finally did me in.

"You want to know what I'm angry about, Lina?" I barreled on, before she could answer. "I'm picking my way through the deadliest woods in the known world for a kingdom that, by all sane accounts, does not exist, and you are perfectly content, because as usual, you aren't thinking about anyone but yourself."

She looked stricken, her tiny fingers fisting around the edge of my pocket.

"That's not—" she started, but I cut her off.

And I knew—I knew—she wasn't really to blame for my foul mood, but somewhere between her indifference at leaving and my inability to shake the constant haunting of the past few months, I couldn't seem to stop myself.

"True? Isn't it, though? Did you ever stop to think about the impossible position you put me in, either letting you traipse off in here to *die*—and let's not kid ourselves, Lina, that's exactly what would have happened—or leave everything on a day's notice to risk my own life for something you have no more than a hunch about?"

She closed her mouth, like even she knew she had nothing to say to that, but somehow the sight just made me more furious.

"Of course you didn't think about me, though. You never have. You never think about the way everyone else has to cater their lives to the way you like to constantly risk yours!" I snapped my mouth shut, because I was coming way too close to saying things I was oath-bound not to say.

She stared up at me, and I realized I had stopped walking somewhere in the middle of my tirade. Her small form was being jostled a bit by the furious way I was huffing out air, but she didn't comment on that.

When she finally did speak, it was only to say three small words.

"Put me down."

I blinked. *Does she not hear a single, damned thing I say about her risking her life?*

"No."

"I always thought you were better than a common bully, Edrich." She sniffled after she said my name, tears pooling into her blue-green eyes, but she didn't sound any less firm. "Don't use your size to force me against my wishes. You don't want to be responsible for my safety, and I don't want your extremely begrudging assistance. So, put me down, walk away, and don't let whether I live or die be your problem anymore."

I laughed. I couldn't help myself.

"It's always my problem, Lina. *You* are always my problem. And no, I won't set you down to die. If you didn't want me responsible for keeping you alive in this troll-begotten forest, you should have thought of that before."

She turned a furious shade of crimson, tiny tears slipping down her cheeks and falling like dew drops onto the fabric of my pocket. Betrayal, hurt, and something else I couldn't quite read flickered across her features and in the shade of her skin in flashes faster than I could follow.

But she wasn't looking up at me like I was her knight in shining armor anymore.

Great. Another mission accomplished.

15

LINA

I was practically vibrating with fury. My skin glowed so fiercely that it illuminated his pocket. I was hurt. And angry. And also... humiliated.

Because beneath the spiteful way he'd said it, his words rang true.

Edrich let out a hiss of pain and muttered a curse about the forsaken hedgehog.

Good. I hope she bit him.

I wiped another angry tear away and tried to still my breathing. I had risked his life. I had expected him to come. But I hadn't realized it was a burden to him... that *I* was a burden to him.

I let that thought sink deeper into my bones, practically severing my heart from my chest.

Am I only a burden to everyone I know? Is that why anyone shows me any kindness? Is it all pretend or pity?

The questions multiplied and swirled around my mind in a vicious loop. I was just Lina. The small girl with the back problems that everyone had to take care of.

I shook my head, trying to rid it of the negativity.

No. I couldn't believe that was true of everyone; but Edrich had made it clear that, at least, he felt that way.

And now we were in the middle of the Enchanted Forest, fighting and unsure of how to move forward.

The anger writhing under my skin gave way completely to sorrow. I wasn't sure how to convince Edrich to leave me here to continue my journey without him, without another argument. And yet, I couldn't stop now.

Taking a deep, steadying breath I turned to face him again.

"Edrich, I—" I began, but he cut me off with a finger to his lips.

His face was ashen, his eyes wide. Somehow in my stewing, I hadn't registered that we'd stopped moving, or that his heart was beating a different, more frantic sort of rhythm behind me.

Somehow, I'd completely missed the way the forest had gone silent—all save for Pepper's *kakking* above. Through the gaps in the trees, there were splashes of green and purple and white making their way toward us.

Edrich spun in a slow circle, revealing that we were completely surrounded. Hooded figures rode atop glistening white horses.

I ducked lower into his pocket, peeking out of the small opening where his button would go.

I rubbed my eyes to make certain I was seeing clearly.

Not horses. They were unicorns with glowing purple-and-green horns and manes.

It was rumored they had died off long ago, but here they were, at least ten of them. A small part of me wanted to hope that if they still lived, then maybe the fairies did, too.

But that feeling fled quickly as I took in their riders. I gulped as the fading light through the forest canopy caught on the sharpened steel the hooded figures brandished. *Steel that is undoubtedly meant for our throats.*

"Well, well, well... what do we have here?" The voice was raspy and hollow, sending shivers down my spine.

"Outsiders." This voice came from our right, and was just as unnerving.

"Supper," said another.

Edrich's body went completely rigid at that. He crossed his arms, and I could feel the tightening of his fists beneath them. When he spoke, his voice held none of the concern I could feel thrumming through his body. Instead, it was a more casual tone that replied to them.

"I don't think that would be such a good idea, but you're welcome to try. You know, if you're desperate."

My heart pounded in my ears, and I nearly collapsed. Surely, he was baiting them. He was probably used to this sort of thing. We'd be fine. *Right?*

A few laughs came from beneath the green hoods, and the unicorns huffed and stomped.

"No? Give us a good reason not to," the first hood spoke, again.

Edrich forced a sigh.

"Do you know what this is?" He pulled out some sort of talisman from around his neck and displayed it to the full circle. It was a bronze circle, inlaid with a sword and shield.

A few of them gasped and looked to their leader before he laughed.

"I see that you do. Then you'll know what I am and that I never travel alone."

A few more chuckles sounded, but they edged closer.

"You may carry the symbol, but you're no real *Huntsman*. We can smell your fear."

Edrich tucked the talisman away and shifted slightly on his feet.

"If that's a risk you're willing to take, then so be it."

This gave them pause, but not for long.

"Explain to us, *boy*, why there is only one set of tracks if you really are part of the Huntsmen?" The speaker paused, before tilting his head. "We think you lie to save your skin."

They inched even closer, before a whirring sounded and Edrich fell to his knees, gasping. He forced himself to stand up, but I could hear the racing of his heart and hear his wheezing breath. *Something is clearly wrong.*

He brought an arm up and, with a sickening sound, he ripped something out of his shoulder. A bloody arrow came into view and I nearly screamed. *They shot him.*

Their hollow voices snickered, a haunting deadly sound that held no joy. Suddenly, Edrich spun around and instead of an arrow, he was holding the sword he kept strapped to his side. He'd moved so fast I hadn't even seen him reach for it.

His blade met that of one of the hooded figures just before theirs could sink down into his chest. Edrich tucked and rolled out of the way of another swordsman that was approaching, and in the movement, I went flying out of his pocket and landed on the mossy ground.

It took me a moment to make the stars stop lining my vision. My chest was tight, and my back ached. I could feel another spasm coming on, while in the background, all I could hear was the sound of metal striking metal.

Then Maggie was next to me, whimpering and nudging me with her snout, trying to make me stand.

At least she seemed unharmed, which was more than I could say for Edrich or myself.

I focused my eyes as best as I could on Edrich's prone form as four hooded figures surrounded him. Before I could stop myself, a guttural scream escaped my lungs.

16

EDRICH

The hoods turned as one at the sound of the scream. I recognized Lina's voice immediately, but until my hand felt my empty pocket, I didn't quite believe it.

I turned my head, my shoulder cursing me in agony with the movement. My eyes frantically searched the forest floor until they found her. She was apparently unharmed. Transfixed, she stared at the spot where blood blossomed from the wound in my shoulder before turning a furious shade of red, so deep it was nearly black, and sparkling with intensity.

Maggie skittered into the bushes behind her as Pepper called out over head.

Gasps sounded from the hooded figures surrounding us as they stepped away, still keeping their weapons drawn. The unicorns stamped their feet with nervous energy, and their riders went eerily still, hesitating for reasons I couldn't understand.

Lina stepped forward, sending them skittering back even further.

Are they afraid of her?

I used their distraction to scramble closer to Lina, just in case one of them decided to trample her.

One of the creatures lunged forward, reaching for me, but another held out a hand to stop him as Lina placed a protective arm in front of me.

How hard have I hit my head?

The image of Lina protecting me seemed so real, but felt so ridiculous, that I brought my good arm up to rub my eyes and clear my vision.

She's still there, as menacing as a four-inch-tall flame.

"It is ill fortune to cross a fairy." The leader's voice sounded distant, and lacked some of the menace from earlier when they were all calling us "supper".

"Are you quite done harassing us?" Lina's voice was firm, and the figures flinched at each word she spoke. "You could've killed us! My friend is bleeding!"

Her color flickered a little, the red dulling ever so slightly.

"We are—" A hood to our left started to speak but another cut him off.

"It is not a real fairy." The one who had reached for me cocked his head to the side as if trying to decide whether or not his assessment was true.

"It doesn't even have wings," one of the others added, looking toward the leader.

"And it's alone," another commented.

They all spoke in hushed tones, their voices haunting, like the wind on a winter's night. Then, all at once, they were inching toward us again. Panic surged in my chest in a fresh new wave.

There was no way even I could defeat all of these creatures. Maybe if I had backup, but the wretched things were right. Not only were we alone, but the other Huntsmen didn't even know where I was.

Outrunning them wasn't an option with a fresh arrow wound. Even if we could make it back to a denser part of the forest where their steeds couldn't follow, we had no idea what else was lurking in these woods.

My mind raced back to the creature with the glowing spines from the other night.

No. *If I can't fight them off, then we will surely die here.*

I nudged Lina toward one of the logs behind me. Maybe she could find shelter before the fighting broke out again. Shifting my legs, I grabbed hold of the dagger in my boot and sent it sailing at one of the creature's heads while they were still preoccupied talking about Lina.

It landed with a sickening thunk, and the rider fell from his unicorn. The others screeched in anger, the sound rattling my bones.

I quickly drew my sword and ran at one of the others, but it deflected my blade easily, knocking me over with a backward shove. Pain shot through me as I rolled over and sprang back up onto my feet. My shoulder throbbed, but I ignored it and took up a defensive position.

"Tell us, child. Why would a lone Huntsman and a half-fairy be wandering the eastern woods?" the attacking figure spoke, its dark, open hood so near my face that I could smell the rot seeping from it.

Like spoiled milk and animal carcasses in the midday sun.

I faked moving to the left, and he fell for it, as I tossed my sword to my good hand and brought it down in an arc across the creature's chest.

Green blood sprayed from the wound as it fell to its knees. Spinning around, I found myself directly in the path of a curved, black blade that was moving toward my neck at an impossible speed.

I had seen death in its many forms, and I had evaded it myself a time or two, but it had never been clearer than it was right now in the form of this evil creature's sword. There was no way I would be able to move in time, not without impaling myself on one of the other blades or horns. *I'm going to die.*

They were going to kill me, and then they were going to kill Lina.

The world spun slowly. I barely registered the sound of Lina's cry while my mind ran through the endless possibilities.

Would Rumplestiltskin let my father die, even if I died protecting Lina? Would that be enough to uphold my end of the bargain?

Somehow, I doubt it.

My last thought was that I would have killed them both, my father and my oldest friend. Then, the blade was inches from my face and there was no more time to think anything at all. I refused to close my eyes. I hadn't looked away from the boy's fate, and I wouldn't look away from mine.

So I saw the exact moment the trajectory of the hit tilted, the sword forcibly yanked back along with its owner. The creature toppled backward, off his vicious beast. Half a heartbeat later, I heard a thwack from directly behind me. I spun in time to see another cloaked figure fall from his unicorn with a dagger protruding from its back.

The leader was turning his evil-horned horse around to charge at whatever was attacking them when the sharp crack of a whip sounded. He clutched at the leather around, what I assumed, was his neck, as it pulled him sideways to the ground.

The others hadn't been able to run fast enough, falling from their unicorns as they tried to escape. I ripped the dagger from the dead body and threw it at one of them when they ran too near to where Lina was hiding.

It cried out as the blade made impact and spun around to face me. With one swift movement, I brought my sword down on its neck and its screeching stopped.

One by one, they all fell.

Their garishly colored steeds wasted no time abandoning them for the woods. I looked around frantically for whatever had killed them, not anxious to meet the creatures capable of such a feat, and my eyes landed on Lina's form, no longer red, but a sickly, horrified pearl and chartreuse. We needed to get out of here.

"Lina," I whispered. "Come on, let's go."

She wasn't looking at me, though. At first, I thought she was staring at one of the fallen bodies, but her gaze was fixed on a shadow a few feet from us. No, not a shadow, I realized. More like... a pocket of darkness. One shaped exactly like the hooded riders.

There are more of them.

17

LINA

I didn't realize that I was shaking until Edrich's warm hands cupped me, pulling me close to his chest.

My arms tightened around his finger, hugging him close to me, as I stared into the darkness between the trees. Not just darkness, but like a black cloud that sucked in whatever light dared to touch it.

Any bravery I'd felt earlier was gone as I stared into the deathly shadows.

I could feel the galloping of Edrich's pulse beneath his skin. Forcing my eyes away from the darkness, I dared to glance up at his face. His features were tight and sickly pale as his shoulder gushed blood at an alarming rate.

My world was spinning out of control. *I can't lose him. I can't be the reason his family never sees him again.*

The shadows between the trees began to quiver until two forms appeared more clearly. It was another hooded rider and another unicorn. Only this one was black and had massive, feathered wings.

Edrich's legs wobbled as he attempted to back further

away from the two approaching figures. Clearing his voice, he started to speak when the rider cut him off.

"You shouldn't be here," he said, removing his hood to reveal pale skin, with long, ebony tresses falling straight down over his shoulders. *An elf.*

His pointed ears twitched, and he looked to the south before sniffing.

The elf muttered something that sounded like a curse in a language I'd never heard before.

"Just let us leave," Edrich said, backing further into the trees in an attempt to put as much distance between us as possible.

"There's no time for that. More of their kind are already on their way."

Edrich and I glanced at each other, then at the forest around us. We had no way of knowing what direction they were coming from, and he was hurt.

"I suppose you'd better follow me," the elf added, picking up Edrich's pack and turning away, heading back into the thicket he came from. "Unless you want to die."

I gulped as Edrich struggled to listen to the forest. I knew he was debating whether or not we would be better off on our own. But when the screaming started, his feet moved forward, toward the dark elf.

Maggie emerged from the bushes and he stopped just quickly enough to scoop her up and put her in the pocket of his cloak, before taking off again.

We moved quickly through the trees. *Or as quickly as we can with Edrich still bleeding so profusely.* I climbed onto his shoulder and applied pressure to the wound as best as I could. He winced but nodded his thanks as we continued our pace.

"This is all my fault," I whispered. "I'm so sorry, Edrich. It's my fault you're hurt."

My stomach twisted into knots. I couldn't bring myself to look at his face, so I wasn't even sure if he'd heard me.

Whether or not he was going to respond was the least of my worries, as more unnerving screaming and wailing came from behind us.

"Just a little further now," the elf said, leading us toward the sound of rushing water.

We picked our way through the trees, following the river as it widened and deepened. The forest was not nearly as dense in this part of the woods. Animal tracks, larger than I'd ever seen, littered the ground at the river-bank. Edrich stepped into them, rather than making fresh ones, following the lead of the mysterious elf and his black steed.

Suddenly, the sound of rushing water was louder than the screaming from behind us, as we rounded a corner and came upon a stunning waterfall.

"Through here." Our leader dismounted his steed and led it around large, mossy rocks—directly behind the curtain of water.

Edrich's steps faltered slightly. His strength was waning, and the blood wouldn't stop pouring from his shoulder.

I pressed harder, and his knees buckled. He only barely caught himself on a mossy rock next to the falls. "Sorry," he muttered.

"No, I'm sorry. I'm so sorry, Edrich." I darted a glance behind us. "It's just a few more feet. You can do this."

Edrich nodded weakly, pushing himself up. His features hardened in determination, and he made the uneasy climb behind the waterfall. His breathing was ragged, his skin slick with a sheen of sweat, but he gingerly placed one foot in front of the other.

The falls were practically roaring to our right, spraying us with water as we inched further behind them.

"That's it. We're almost there." I whispered encouragement in his ear, as a flash of white flew past us.

Pepper.

I had no reason to trust the man who led us here, other than my gut. Somehow, deep down, I knew he wasn't a threat. Not to us, at least. Or maybe I was just blindly hoping for the best, again.

"Not much farther now," I repeated to Edrich.

"Lina?" Edrich's voice was hoarse.

"Yes? What is it?" Dread pooled in my stomach.

"How would you know how much further it is? Just... just stop talking."

I was not sure whether to laugh or be offended. But if Edrich could summon the energy to be grouchy again, then maybe he would be okay, after all.

A moment later, we rounded a corner into a large, cavernous space. Pepper was perched high up on an opening in the cave wall, her head tilting toward us as we made our way in.

The elf was already making a fire; a pot of clean water, and what looked like fresh bandages, were nearby.

"See, I was right!" I squeaked, relieved that we could soon clean his wounds, and hoping that the mortar and pestle next to the stranger was something that might help Edrich.

"Yes, Lina. You're always ri—" the ground raced up to

meet us, cutting his words off entirely, as he hit the cave floor with a thud.

Two hands reached out to gently catch me and Maggie. I thought it was Edrich for a moment, before realizing that it was the stranger. He had somehow been fast enough to cross the six yards to get to us before we were thrown across the cavern or crushed under Edrich.

I didn't have time to be relieved or grateful for his help. Not when my eyes landed on my oldest friend's pale, unmoving form lying on the wet stone ground.

❧ 18 ❧

EDRICH

"Edrich?"

I expected to awake to the same darkness and pain that had claimed me, but, instead, a familiar voice lulled me gently into consciousness. For a moment, I thought I was back on the farm, then I caught the earthy scent of damp rocks and another acrid odor I couldn't place.

My eyes flew open, instantly on alert.

"Edrich?" Lina said my name again, her cool hand on my temple like she was trying to infuse me with some of the light and life she carried with her everywhere she went.

Or maybe my head is just fuzzy from passing out.

"I'm up," I said gruffly, sitting up to survey our surroundings and get a good look at our unlikely savior.

And maybe to put some distance between Lina and me.

The flapping of wings pulled my attention away from her, and I caught sight of Pepper perched on a lip of the cave wall. She was contentedly grooming herself and didn't seem to be too wary of the situation we had found ourselves in.

I tucked that away. She was usually very good at judging whether or not there was danger nearby.

My eyes darted toward the dark man sitting in the corner, his shadowy-winged unicorn looking no less intimidating, even though it was crunching on an apple, then down at my freshly bandaged shoulder wound. That's where the pungent odor was coming from, but I would take a smell over the white-hot pain any day.

"Thank you," I told him.

He only surveyed me a moment before nodding. Whatever the creatures we had fought were, this man didn't appear to be exactly the same.

But he wasn't entirely different, either.

Now that he had pushed back his hood, I could see his skin was pulled just a little too tight over his sharply angled bones, and there was a predatory grace in the way he moved that even those skilled enough to be in the Huntsmen hadn't exhibited. He was an elf, probably, but unlike any I'd seen before.

"Ucafre says we can stay the night here," Lina spoke up.

I could only assume Ucafre was the elf's name.

When his gaze turned to her, something in his midnight eyes softened. I would have laughed if it wouldn't have tugged at my fresh wound. *How did she manage to win everyone and everything over?*

"That's very kind," I said, honestly. Clearly if he wanted to hurt us, he would have.

"What did those men want from us?" Lina's voice was strained.

Ucafre laughed, but the sound was without humor.

"Women, you mean," he added, with a shake of his head. "They are wraiths, and they are female, and they likely wanted to eat you."

Lina gulped, her rapidly changing skin color pulsating and glowing in the dark cave. Her hedgehog snuggled next to her, to either offer comfort or take it.

"Do you have any advice for evading the wraiths going forward?" I asked.

He fixed me with another long stare, unblinking and eerily expressionless, before he answered.

"They cannot cross the water," he said, gesturing toward the river just beyond the waterfall.

Relief flooded me, but he wasn't finished.

"However, they are hardly the most dangerous thing in this forest."

"Of course not." Lina practically sparkled up at him. "You're more dangerous than they are."

He shook his head at her, but not unkindly.

"No, little wingless fairy." He said it almost affectionately. "I happened upon them when they were weak— tired. They usually hunt at night, so whatever circumstance brought them to you during the day worked in your favor, but don't be fooled. Things here are not as they are in your part of the world, and anything that can afford to stand out in this forest is deadly."

I swallowed a little at his sobering words, but Lina only seemed to hear one thing.

"Fairy? Does that mean they're real? You've seen people like me?"

He nodded, reluctantly. "More or less," he said.

"But they have wings. And I don't." Her shoulders sagged, her color turning blue. "So I really am alone." She whispered the last bit more to herself than to either of us.

Her words sliced at something inside me for reasons I couldn't quite explain. Before I could process that, she squared her shoulders, her skin reverting back to rose-gold.

"No, I can't believe that. Even if I'm not a real fairy, if I'm not from here, surely they'll still know more about me than I do."

I was unreasonably envious of the way she managed to face everything with that relentless spirit of hers. I had always assumed it was the kind of false confidence you developed when you led a life as sheltered as hers had been, but her mother had died, and her best friend had abandoned her, and she was still going strong.

Lately, I was not so sure I had ever really known her at all. *I've never even realized how unhappy she's been all these years.*

"Here." The man placed a wooden bowl in front of me, pulling me from those thoughts. "This is a *bloodshroom.*"

I had certainly survived on worse than the slimy red mushrooms he presented me, but that didn't make them much more appealing. At my hesitation, he spoke up again.

"No, they aren't toxic, and they contain no actual blood, if that's what you're wondering. They are simply fortified with iron, and will help you regain what you've lost."

For an unreasonable moment, I thought he was talking about something else entirely. *What I've lost.* My gaze slid to Lina before I chastised myself internally. She was right here. I hadn't lost her.

Not yet, anyway.

Belatedly, I put the two things he had said together, though, and realized he was talking about my physical blood loss.

Sweet fairy hell, I needed to get some sleep.

19

LINA

E drich's normal coloring began to trickle back in, slowly. The more of the disgusting-looking mushrooms he ate, the less pale he seemed. I felt as if I had been holding my breath since our encounter with those creatures, and when I finally released it, I was almost dizzy.

I had been ignoring my back spasms, forcing myself to be all right until I knew Edrich was safe. With the exhaustion from the day, and the relief that we'd live through the night crashing in, it left no more energy for me to fight the pain.

I paced near the fire and tried to focus on anything else, on everything else.

"Earlier, you said you have seen fairies?" I asked, hoping that the fear and adrenaline from earlier would dull me once more.

Ucafre nodded sagely.

"Where? When?" I needed to know everything he knew. I needed to know that we were on the right path.

"It has been some time. They keep to themselves in the North Woods," Ucafre answered, studying my pacing form. "They do not take well to outsiders, though."

He looked up at Edrich with his last comment, and I couldn't decide what his motives were. *Are he and I both outsiders in this equation?*

"They are the only lead I have... the only possibility that I know of to find out where I came from. I have to find them—" I cut my last word off abruptly, sucking in a sharp breath.

The pain was darting up and down my spine so forcefully, for a moment, I forgot how to breathe.

"Lina?" Edrich's voice was hesitant. "Are you all right?"

I was about to open my mouth to respond to him when the spasm in my back became too much.

"Peonies!" I gasped, nearly falling to my knees.

"What has happened?" Ucafre asked, moving closer.

I opened my mouth to speak, but a cry escaped me instead. I crumpled to the ground, pain lancing up and down my back so fiercely that I saw actual stars blooming in front of me and blinding my vision.

Maggie ran over to comfort me, lifting me up with her nose.

"Lina. This is more than you led on. What is going on? What is wrong?" Edrich's voice was riddled with concern.

"My back," I croaked out, curling up into a ball.

Edrich muttered a string of curses, and I barely made out the questions Ucafre was asking, let alone form the answers. My back throbbed and cracked and seemed to be splitting down the middle.

Tears streamed down my face as I desperately tried to breathe through the pain. Edrich's words were clipped when he explained the spasms that had assaulted me from infancy, much to the intrigue of Ucafre. At some point, I tuned them out entirely, succumbing to the pain and hearing only Magnolia's gentle whines in my ear.

Being in so much pain only made me miss Mama more. When I thought of the way she would soothe me, help me work through them, comfort me—it hurt even worse than the physical pain.

The well of grief opening up inside of me threatened to swallow me whole. If she had not died... If she were still here...

Suddenly, Edrich's voice was louder, breaking through my downward spiral as he argued with the elf. Ucafre's voice was calmer, but no less insistent, even though I couldn't quite make out their words. I stretched toward Maggie's bag that held my ointment.

But it was not there. When I had changed my clothes earlier, it must have fallen out.

Before I could crawl around and look for it, warm hands were picking me up, and Edrich's voice was in my ear.

"I am going to put this medicine on your back. I have to lift your shirt." His voice was riddled with uncertainty, but I nodded in agreement.

If he had found my medicine, I wouldn't be so proud as to not let him apply it. *I need something, anything, to make the pain stop.*

Slowly, carefully, he lifted my shirt, and his finger rubbed a pungent-smelling substance on my back. It wasn't my ointment, but its effects were undeniable.

The pain went from searing and white hot to throbbing, and eventually to something more tolerable.

When I could finally take deep, even breaths without wincing, I knew the worst was over. Judging by the look on Edrich's face, I wasn't sure which of us was more relieved by that.

"Are you all right?" he asked.

He was still cradling me gently in his hands.

I sighed, bleary-eyed and light-headed. With the pain ebbing away, exhaustion swooped in.

"Yes. I think it's over," I said, sheepishly.

Edrich seemed to relax at that, until Ucafre spoke, at least.

"The herbs help mitigate the pain, but depending on the wound, the healing process can be quite brutal." He studied me for a moment. "How long have you had these spasms?"

"As long as I can remember."

"I thought you said they went away years ago, that you were better." Edrich's tone was accusatory.

"Well," I responded. "They didn't. And I am not."

Edrich stiffened. While his color didn't give away his feelings, I could read his expression clearly. He was disappointed, maybe even angry with me. *Again.*

Ucafre cleared his throat, nodding at whatever thought that came to him, and made his excuses. Pointing to a bedroll by the fire, he assured us that we were welcome until morning, and that he would be sleeping in the adjacent alcove of the cave.

Edrich didn't say much in response. Putting me down, he quietly unrolled the blankets, setting up his bed for the night.

I decided to do the same with my roll, losing myself in my own thoughts in the process.

Every move I made was illuminated by a soft blue light, my emotions on full display in the darkness. Maggie followed me around until I found a spot close enough to the fire to stay warm, but far enough away not to swelter.

Taking her small bit of cloth, she rolled around until she was sufficiently wrapped in it. It wasn't long before her nose was buried under her scrap of blanket and she was snoring.

If only it was that easy for me...

My mind ran wild with a million scenarios for how differently the day could've gone. I had hoped this whole thing would be one last adventure for Edrich and me. That maybe it would heal the rift between us... but instead, I had almost gotten him killed.

All for what? To find a people that I may not even belong to?

What have I done?

20

EDRICH

S leep was never going to come. Not when Lina was lying there like a tiny beacon of pain. Besides, Ucafre's imposing presence may have been enough to frighten away the other predators in the forest, but the smaller critters could kill Lina as easily as the large ones.

That is the reason I gave myself when I sighed audibly, getting her attention. Not because she was a deeper, grayer blue than I had ever seen, the color flaring brightly with waves of pain, and what I suspected were sobs.

No, this is only about her safety.

"Lina, why have you put your—" Was it really a sleep roll when it could fit around my thumb? It was for her, I supposed. "Sleep roll so far from mine?"

She had her back to me, so I only saw her stand up to pull her sleeping roll a couple feet closer to mine. Well, at least she was within arm's reach to protect her now.

She lay back down without a word.

Over the years, I had begun to understand her color

system a little better. The color itself represented a base emotion, then she would glow with the intensity of it.

Right now... blue meant sadness. But the way it shone so brightly it cast sparkly shadows on the wall, that went far beyond feeling a little down. *This is grief.*

Even if I hadn't known her colors, any idiot could have figured that much out from the sob she had just let out.

"Lina?" I finally spoke, again. "Do you want to tell me what's wrong?"

"Everything," she whispered. "Me. I'm wrong. Not quite a fairy. Not quite anything else." She sniffled. "And then there's you." Her voice got louder, and I braced myself.

The list of things wrong with me was plenty long. But she surprised me, looking up at me with her water-filled eyes.

"I could have watched you die today, just like I watched—" She cut off before she could say her mother, but it still felt like being stabbed with a barbed poker, knowing she had hurt like that. Imagining her minuscule form hovering near the unmoving body of the unbelievably kind woman who had raised her, no one around to offer comfort.

Or maybe someone had been around, and it just hadn't been me. For that matter, my family had probably been there, probably some of her friends. Neira and Vale. For some reason, that last thought made me scowl.

It's a wonder she doesn't hate me.

I reached out to comfort her, even though it was weeks too late, but she pulled back.

"It would have been all my fault," she sobbed.

"Lina, no." I looked directly at her, willing her to see

the truth in my words. "I chose to come into this forest, knowing full well what it had in store. Or, at least the stories of it. That would not have been your fault."

"But I'm the one who asked you to come." She sniffled.

"But I'm the one who said yes," I insisted.

She raised her chin a little, her tears slowly ebbing away, though she was still a solid, shimmering blue.

"I'm sure you think I'm ridiculous for—" She gestured to her face.

I shook my head, the effects of the blood loss and exhaustion making me more honest than usual.

"For being brave in the face of the most terrifying creatures I've ever seen? For going after what most people thought was nothing more than legend, only to find out you were right? Or for keeping yourself together, no matter what the day threw at us? No, Lina, I don't think you're ridiculous because you took a moment to cry at the end of all that."

Finally, her skin moved to a pale rose-gold, effectively zapping the light from the cave.

"Thank you." Her voice was quieter than usual in the darkness.

"For what?" I asked.

"For saying all of that. For being my friend." She paused before adding, "For coming out here with me even though you had nothing to gain from it."

I felt like I had been kicked in the gut. Even if I hadn't been bound by oath not to tell her the truth, that I had plenty to gain from coming with her—or at least, plenty to lose if I didn't—I couldn't have gotten the words out just then.

"Of course," I finally bit out, but my voice was hollow.

Would I have come anyway? Our relationship was so tangled up by over a decade of obligation and confusion that I couldn't be sure of the answer, and that was the worst part of it all.

21

LINA

It wasn't long after I closed my eyes that it was already morning.

Ucafre was making a small breakfast at the newly-lit fire. Eggs of some sort with an array of vegetables and mushrooms. It was delicious and savory and just what I needed after a fitful night of sleep.

But none of it compared to the steaming cup of hazelnut tea. Just the smell of it made me feel warm and cozy and almost as if yesterday's events hadn't happened at all.

Almost.

My eyes were still red and swollen from crying so much, and I would be lying if I said I wasn't a little embarrassed. I stretched up on my tiptoes to take another sip of warm tea from the wooden cup, letting it soothe my frazzled mind.

"How is your back this morning, little fairy?" Ucafre asked.

I stretched and rolled my shoulders before shaking my

head back and forth. "Still a little tight, but much better. Thank you."

He nodded and took another drink from his cup.

"Ucafre?"

"Yes?"

"Do you think we'll find the fairies?" I felt Edrich's quizzical glance, but he kept silent.

I wasn't even sure why I was asking. I needed to believe that we would find them, or all of this would've been for nothing... *And I'm not sure that's something I could live with.*

Ucafre sighed, his expression turning thoughtful.

"It is not impossible. It is more a matter of whether or not they want to be found." I felt myself deflate a little, but he wasn't finished. "However, I cannot imagine them not wanting to be found by you."

Edrich picked me up to rest on his shoulder, his body rigid and tense.

"Thank you, Ucafre." He reached out to shake his hand.

"Keep to the edges of the forest, if you can, and follow the river north until you pass the purple hills. That is where I last saw a fairy," Ucafre said, shaking hands with Edrich and dipping his head toward me before mounting his steed.

"Thank you," I echoed, smiling up at him.

He nodded and pulled on the reins of his black unicorn. The magnificent creature mirrored the gesture, and they turned to walk in the opposite direction.

Edrich cleared his throat and scooped up a prickly Maggie, placing her in his satchel before exiting the other side of the waterfall to avoid walking through the river.

With Ucafre's instructions, he didn't need my map or guidance, and it wasn't long before we were once again silently on our way.

AFTER TWO HOURS of quietly trekking through the forest, my nerves and back were once again tense. No matter how much stretching I did, I couldn't seem to get comfortable. The pain had become a dull ache, but it was still there.

I tried laying on my back, bent over his shoulder—I tried laying on my stomach. I tried twisting and turning and sitting cross-legged until I was going to lose my mind from it all.

Until a small blessed ray of sunlight reflected off of the flask in Edrich's backpack. Quickly untangling it from the straps that held it in place, I shook the thing, delighted by the weight of spirits it still contained. I'd always been stronger than my height should've allowed for, so lifting the full flask wasn't difficult. Just awkward.

Twisting open the cap, the smell of whiskey made my eyes water.

Thank the stars.

I gingerly lifted the flask up and savored each delicious drop, careful not to slosh any out.

"What are you doing back there?" Edrich's voice nearly made me drop the precious container of booze.

"Ah, he speaks," I said, before I could help myself.

His head tilted to the side, and I could imagine the sarcastic smirk on his mouth.

"You haven't been very talkative yourself."

Fair.

I chugged the whiskey until the flask was light enough to carry back up to his shoulder.

Edrich sniffed and laughed.

"Really, Lina? You're just going to help yourself to my stash without offering to share?"

"Sorry?" I smiled, and handed him the flask.

"No, you're not." He took a swig.

He shook the canteen and tilted his head before handing it back.

"I always forget how strong you are. This was full this morning. Even half empty, it still weighs more than you."

"Indeed. It is one of life's great mysteries. Like how the bumblebee can fly or how ants can lift far, far more than their bodies should allow," I said, before taking another long drink.

He snorted.

"Ah, yes... you are shrouded in mystery." He laughed, then. "I'm not sure how I could forget the way you snuck bottles of wine from your mother's pantry that were easily five times your size, bottles we weren't even supposed to know were there. You just carried them around like it was nothing."

"Hey, you helped."

"I would never steal." He feigned innocence, and I flicked his ear. "But also, it would have been irresponsible to let you drink it all by yourself."

Edrich laughed again, and somehow the sound made me homesick. It reminded me of a different version of him. A younger, and less burdened version of him.

"I like when you laugh. You seem more like *you* when you do."

I felt his body tense as he let out a small snort, but said nothing in response.

The more whiskey I drank, the less I noticed the agitation in my body and soul. Propping my back up against his neck, I stretched out my legs over his shoulder and watched the trees go by in a blur of colors.

"If we are going to continue to be silent, at least the views aren't bad."

"Which view are you talking about, Lina? The back of my head? Or the dark and depressing forest we're hiking through?"

I giggled, the whiskey making me feel a little light-headed.

"I was talking about the forest. It may be dark, but look at the way the mushrooms on the trees glow, or the way the small rays of light reflect off of the white leaves, making them look like giant snowflakes. This place is beautiful, Edrich. I wish you could see that."

He chuckled and shook his head.

"But," I added, after a moment, "you're not half bad to look at, either."

Edrich cleared his throat uncomfortably.

"How much of that bourbon have you had?"

I handed him the empty flask, and he groaned.

"Curses, Lina! That stuff is potent."

"I know." I responded with a giggle. "It did the trick quite nicely."

22

EDRICH

As the medicine on my shoulder wore off, the pain gradually returned. It wasn't as sharp as before, though, just a steady ache that throbbed with each step.

Fortunately, Lina was providing quite a distraction from that.

She sat cross-legged on my good shoulder now, her head in her hands, gazing up at me with what might have been amusement. I wasn't sure. It was hard to read her colors when she was flashing through them fast enough to give me a seizure. Most of them I recognized, but a few had surprised me lately.

"Lina?" I might as well ask her about them since we had literally nothing better to do.

Besides, my shoulder wound wasn't the only thing I needed a distraction from.

All my life, I had believed the fairies were a myth... Lina had just been Lina. But now, she was right, and they were real. Every step we walked brought us one step closer to that world, and one step closer to her being... gone.

I shouldn't care when I was the one who never came home. It was selfish of me, really, to just assume she would be waiting on her farm for the moment when I finally decided to bother to head back there. *But there it is.*

"Edrich?" She had been saying my name, I realized.

I cleared my throat, trying to remember what I was going to ask her. She flashed a deep shade of shimmering purple, reminding me.

"Right. I know most of your colors, but there are a few I'm still not sure about."

"Like which ones?"

"Purple?" I asked.

The purple morphed into a fuchsia, and that one I did know. *Embarrassment.*

"Um, I'm not really sure. I'm not always looking at myself, you know," she rambled. "You said a few. What others?"

I chuckled, causing her to turn purple again, before I asked the next one.

"Green?"

"Oh, that one's easy. That light green color usually means I'm feeling pukey." She laughed, a bubbling sound that seemed to light up the forest itself.

"But what about dark green?"

She went fuchsia again.

"That just means I'm feeling... really pukey," she said, after a minute.

"I see." I nodded, waiting for her color to ebb back to normal before adding, "Hey, Lina?"

"Yeah?"

"You're a terrible liar." She always had been.

She brought her hands up to her face, giggling a bit.

"How about... I ask you a question, instead."

"Well, that hardly seems fair," I said, laughing under my breath.

"I promise to answer yours after."

"Also unfair. This feels like when we were kids and you always wanted to play princess dress-up, but you insisted on making me play the ogre."

"To be fair, that was before I met any ogres."

"It wasn't the ogre I was concerned about." I shook my head at her line of thinking.

"So, my question," she started.

"I can see there's no reasoning with you here, so by all means, go ahead," I said, like it would make a difference.

I was, admittedly, curious what ridiculousness she was wondering about in that head of hers, at this point.

"Have you ever thought about what our lives would have been like if we were the same size?"

I stopped dead in my tracks, belatedly reaching a hand up so she didn't pitch forward into a tree. *Of all the things I expected her to ask, this was not one of them.*

"Sorry, I thought I saw something," I lied, picking up the pace again.

"You didn't answer my question," she reminded me.

"Oh, right. Um, I guess not really," I lied, again.

"Hey, Edrich?"

"Yeah, Lina?"

"You're an even worse liar than I am."

I didn't answer her, not just because I didn't want to admit it, but also because my mind was suddenly spinning about three years backward.

"Edrich." My mother's tone was soft, but firm. "How will you find a wife if you spend all your time with Lina?"

"I don't want a wife, Mama," I insisted. "No one's ever going to get me like she does, anyway."

"I see," she sighed. "And does she feel the same way?"

"I... don't know," I admitted.

"Then maybe now would be the time to walk away before it gets even harder."

"What?" I looked up, surprised. My mother loved Lina, but more than that, she knew why I could never leave her side.

"You've been burdened by this oath for too long. We will make sure Lina is safe. You know that I adore her, but I think you need distance to see this situation more clearly."

"Distance isn't going to change how I feel." I shook my head.

She put a hand on my shoulder, and I covered it with my own.

"I hope that isn't true, because I love you, Edrich, and I love her, and I want what's best for you both. And a life where you can never have a family, have children, or even the comfort of one another's arms... that's not what's best for either of you."

"I don't care about those things." I was fighting to stay calm, but the truth of her words was hitting like a battering ram.

"Not for yourself, maybe, but what about for Lina? We still don't know who she is or where she comes from. If someone her size comes along someday, will she really thank you for tying her down to the kind of half-life you're talking about?"

I sank into one of the wooden kitchen chairs. Was that how Lina would see it? Being tied down by me? If there was even a chance of that, was my mother right? Would it be better to spare us both?

Three days later, Atesh had come—my father had mentioned my skill with animals, and he was in need of a falconer. I had followed my mother's advice and gone with him, but I had been right, in the end. *Time hasn't changed how I feel.*

"It means jealousy." Lina's slightly too loud voice in my ear startled me out of my thoughts. "Dark green," she added.

"Why didn't you want to admit that?"

"Ah ah ah." She wagged her finger at me. "You don't get another question when you never really answered mine."

"I did, too," I said.

"Lies!" She practically shouted, before melting into a fit of drunken giggles, again.

"Fine! Yes, Lina, I thought about it. We were together all the time. Of course I thought about it. Hell, there was a time that was pretty much all I did."

Well, that had been more truth than I meant to give her, but it was out there now, in the forest that suddenly felt far too quiet in the wake of Lina's stunned silence.

"Oh," she finally said, her voice more sober than before. "Well. I thought about it, too."

We were done talking for a while after that, which was just as well. I was pretty sure I knew what purple meant, and I didn't actually think either of us needed the added tension of her saying it out loud. I sighed.

It really is too bad she had finished off my flask.

❧ 23 ❧

LINA

Even in my bourbon stupor, I was still reeling a bit from everything Edrich had just said. He hadn't meant it. He couldn't have. That would be impossible.

Right?

My mind spun with the implications of it all as I watched the fading beams of sunlight wink away in the canopy above us. When it became too dark to go any further, Edrich set up camp for us, this time making use of tree branches along with bits of the torn canvas he had left.

"You really are spectacular." I sighed, staring up at him in awe.

His hands stilled from where he was tying the branches together, and he laughed.

"You're drunk, Lina."

My expression morphed to one of mock offense, and he laughed again. It hit me how much I would miss this when we reached the fairies. That thought felt too sobering at the moment, though, so I forced it away and went back to generally admiring the man in front of me.

"I'm not drunk." I hiccupped. "But it is true. I saw the way that woman looked at you at the tavern. I'm sure you have conquests all over the countryside."

Edrich's grip slipped, and some of the branches he'd been holding flipped back and hit him in the face.

"Frakking Fairies, Lina!" His tone was flustered as he tried to gain control over his contraption again. "Why would you say that? No, I do not have *conquests* up and down the countryside, thank you very much."

"Well, how would I know that? It's not like you talk to me about your personal life." I laughed, but I couldn't deny the small part of me that felt relief to know I was wrong. *Hopefully*.

"Well, I can promise you that if it were true, it's definitely not a conversation I would be having with you."

"Why not? If we're friends and all, don't I deserve to know about the girl who might have claimed your heart?" I cringed internally at my own boldness.

Why do I even want to know? His relationships weren't my business, but something in me hoped he answered, anyway.

Edrich cleared his throat and shook his head.

"There is no one, Lina." Then more quietly, under his breath. "There hasn't been anyone in a very long time."

For several moments, everything around us disappeared until his attention turned back to the branches he was tying together. There was a tension in the air that pulsed with honesty I wasn't bold enough to dwell on, even in my inebriated state.

"Where did you learn this?" I asked, changing the

subject.

I walked around our shelter for the night, admiring the way he'd made use of mud and leaves and canvas to come up with a tent of sorts.

"Oh." His voice was more resigned than it had been a moment ago. "It's just something I picked up."

A small laugh escaped me.

"I've known you my whole life, and I never knew you had a secret talent for—"

"Can we just drop it?" His tone was sharp.

I felt myself deflate. *How did we go from laughing and whatever else just happened to anger?*

He cast a sideways glance my way, then sighed before answering, like he was deflating a bit, as well.

"I learned it in my training." Something in his voice was distant and sad, and it brought back to mind what he had said in the woods when we were being attacked, what he had shown them.

"As a Huntsman?" I asked, cautiously.

His features were like solid granite now, and he barely got out a small dip of his head in confirmation.

"Why is that such a bad thing that you felt like you couldn't even tell me?" My voice was quiet. I didn't want him to shut me out again, but I also didn't understand why he would keep his job a secret from me. "Aren't they pretty elite?" I pushed when he didn't respond. "Isn't that something to be proud of?"

His shoulders tensed while he dug around in his bag for something before finally pulling out the medallion he had shown the wraiths. Shaking his head, he met my probing gaze with his own somber one.

"There was a time I thought so."

24

EDRICH

I grasped the symbol of my pledge to the Huntsmen, my fingers running mechanically over the sword and shield that were meant to symbolize the balance between the protection and power we had to offer, while I considered her question.

"How much do you know about the Huntsmen?" I asked.

"Not much," she admitted. "Just that it's a band of highly trained soldiers."

"Mercenaries," I corrected, in a dark tone.

"Isn't that... basically the same thing?" Her brow furrowed.

It would have been bad enough if she had understood what I was, but having to explain it to her was a thousand times worse. She looked up at me, her eyes wary but questioning, and her skin still flashing between muted and shimmering colors with every breath.

I pinched the bridge of my nose between two fingers.

"Sometimes, it feels that way. And then sometimes,

mercenaries take the jobs no one wants to talk about—the ones the soldiers are too honorable to take." This was already creeping into territories I had no intention of telling anyone about, let alone her. *It's bad enough that I have to live with the things I've done without parading them around.*

"But... you're honorable." She said it like she was confused, because clearly I fit in that former category. Like it would never even occur to her that a person can be more than one thing, or that maybe I wasn't everything she thought I was.

For some reason, it made me unreasonably angry. At her. At myself. *At life.*

"You asked why I didn't want to tell you, Lina. This is why!" I threw my hands up, my temper overpowering the sense I had to stay quiet in these woods. "You've been alive just as long as I have, but you let yourself be blind to what other people have no choice but to see."

She sat up straighter, her eyes boring into me with accusation. "Or maybe that's just a convenient excuse for you to keep me in the dark whenever you feel like it. How can you expect me to know something I've never been told?"

"Maybe I would have told you if I felt like you could handle it," I snapped.

I wanted to take the words back as soon as they left my lips, even before she turned a deep, glittering red, nearly as dark as she had been when the wraiths attacked. *Rage.*

"Oh, you were worried about my handling of it?" Her voice was harsher than I'd ever heard it. "Like you were worried about how I *handled* you up and leaving without a word? Like you were worried about how I *handled* my mother's death? I've seen the letters you send your family,

Edrich. I know you're perfectly capable of stringing more than five words together on a sheet of paper, but that's all I warranted on either of those occasions?"

I fought to keep my face from coloring with a mixture of anger and shame, because there was so much she didn't know or understand... but then, she wasn't wrong, either.

"*I had to leave.*" She parroted back the words on the first note I ever left her. "Four words that explained exactly nothing. *I'm sorry for your loss.*" She sounded even more enraged at the note I had sent to her mother's funeral. "Five words you would say to a stranger, about a stranger, not to your best friend about her mother, the woman who made you pastries and adored you like her own son!" Tears pooled in her eyes, a few escaping down her cheeks.

And for some reason, that made the anger win out over shame. Maybe I resented her for being able to ignore her feelings when I felt everything in such stark, unrelenting clarity, or maybe I just wanted to see her for a change when the barriers were down, to know I wasn't the only one suffering.

"Well, at least you finally said something real," I said. "How long have you been holding that in, Lina, shoving it down and pretending it didn't exist?"

Somehow, it felt like that last question meant more than my brain was willing to admit it did.

"You want to hear something real?" Her teal eyes pierced mine with intensity. "*You. Left. Me.*"

And some part of me had thought it hadn't really bothered her until she hurled it at me now.

"I thought we were best friends," she choked out. "Together, every day, then you vanished without even popping over to say goodbye on your way out. So, since you've made it painfully clear that the role I have to play in your life is essentially *nothing*, you can go home now. I'll find the fairies from here."

"Nothing?" I barely choked the word out. "My entire life has been about you since I was ten years old!" My words cut off rapidly, because I was coming dangerously close to revealing things I was bound by oath not to tell her. I switched gears. "And we're in this now, Lina. Turning back isn't a luxury I have. So as much as you love to hide from all of your problems, I'm afraid this is one time you'll just have to deal with it."

Her color darkened to a deep burgundy, glittering so fiercely, it was hard to look at her. Without another word, she spun on her heels and stalked off into the makeshift tent. Just before she slipped through the opening, she called over her shoulder.

"You're so right. I can't believe I've been hiding from my problems all this time when I could have been handling them in the mature, sensible way that you do." She turned her head just far enough to glare at me. "Running away."

THE SUN WAS SETTING, and I was seriously weighing the risk of sleeping out here with whatever beasts roamed the forest against the frustration of facing Lina and her random spewing of uncomfortable truths in the tent.

If nothing else, at least I don't have to go in right now.

No sooner had the thought crossed my mind than a rustling sound had me grasping the hilt of my sword. It was halfway out of the sheath before a familiar green-scaled figure appeared, swirling ocher eyes looking angrier than I'd ever seen them—an effect that wasn't lessened by the fact that he was only about as tall as my waist these days.

Rumplestiltskin.

"What are you doing here?" I asked him.

"No," he snarled, revealing a mouth of sharp, golden teeth. "The question is, what are *you* doing here? More importantly, what is *she* doing here?"

Then, he stilled, his eyes darting around furiously. "Where is she?"

I stared him down while I replayed my conversation with Lina, about how I didn't respect her enough to answer her questions. Maybe it was true, to some extent. I could have tried harder to let her know what was going on.

I can't go back and fix that, but I can start now.

"She stormed off after we fought." I stuck to the truth, knowing he could sniff out a lie like a bloodhound.

"You let her leave?" he hissed.

"She's an adult," I reminded him. "I didn't *let* her do anything."

"You're supposed to be protecting her." There was no mistaking the threat in his tone.

"That's why I came with her." I made sure he knew I hadn't broken our deal.

"You call gallivanting off with her into the most dangerous forest known to man, or beast, protection? Then, you just let her waltz off without even bothering to look for her?" He shook his head, his eyes burning with a lethal quality. "We made a *deal,* boy. You protect her, I keep your father alive. Did you somehow manage to forget that with that thick skull of yours, or did you just decide you don't care anymore?"

I seethed at his implication, but my voice was calm when I spoke, only addressing one part of what he had said. "I didn't look for her, because I didn't need to."

Rumplestiltskin was nothing if not shrewd. A rare look of horror crossed his features while he turned slowly to see what I had already noticed. Lina was standing behind him.

And she had heard everything.

25

LINA

The momentary relief of seeing Uncle alive after months and months of no word was completely replaced by something else entirely.

Fury. And worse, something that felt like slimy creatures were crawling through my insides. *Betrayal.*

As angry as I had been at Edrich, I was now also furious on his behalf—on his entire family's behalf.

"Is it true?" The words escaped my lips before I had time to decide if I wanted the answer. "Uncle, is it true that you held his father's life over his head—for me?"

I looked between the two most important men in my life for an answer that neither seemed to be willing to give. Uncle rubbed a hand over his face, and Edrich stared down at him with a grim sort of triumph.

I shook my head, and my whole body seemed to twitch and tingle. The cool night air, and even colder atmosphere with the two men, had me shivering.

"Answer me!" I shouted, startling them both. "Tell me the truth. For once in my life, someone tell me what is actually going on." I could only imagine how ridiculous I looked, shouting at the two men in only my thin, sleeveless nightgown, in the middle of this forsaken forest.

But I don't care. My skin glowed the deepest shade of ruby I'd ever felt, and I lit up the entire area like a beacon of anger.

Maggie appeared at my side, her wet nose pressing into my palm to comfort me, but I pulled it away. I didn't want to be comforted. I didn't want to calm down. I wanted the truth. Though a twinge of guilt nipped at me when her sad, spiky form retreated into the tent, I didn't reach for her.

I was close to shouting again when Uncle finally released a sigh.

"It isn't as simple as that, Little One. There were other factors involved."

I glanced up at Edrich to see the anger light up his eyes.

"She already heard you, Rumple. You may as well be honest now," he added, and Uncle turned on him.

"Yes, what a clever game you've played, mercenary. If I believed you had the brains for it, I'd think you had set this up on purpose." He spat the words with fury, his golden teeth shining behind a vicious sneer. "That you had betrayed your oath, and that I have no further need to honor my part."

"I have done nothing but fulfill my oath to you. I have protected her. My family has protected her. We have spent our lives keeping her safe. And I never told her, as I swore I wouldn't. *You* just did." Edrich's voice was steely calm. "Will you go back on *your* word when we've done nothing but keep ours?"

While his words sounded angry, there was unfiltered fear in his eyes. Uncle's lips turned up into a vile grin, but before he could respond, I found myself shouting instead.

"Enough!" I felt another twitch on either side of my spine, then warmth washing down my back. The spasms were threatening to return, but I ignored the pain.

I ignored everything but the horrible reality of my entire world turning upside down in the last few minutes. Uncle wasn't who I thought he was, and anything Edrich or his family felt for me had been a complete lie in an effort to keep his father alive.

I couldn't blame him for that. I couldn't blame anyone for that, for wanting someone you love to live. *But it still changes things.*

"Enough," I said again, more quietly.

A torrent of emotions ran through me, fast as lightning. My heart hammered within my breast, and I squeezed my eyes shut against it all. Against every word and memory.

"Lina." Uncle's voice was hesitant; the malice it held for Edrich was gone. "You need to calm down, Little One. You're going to have another—"

"No! No more. No more pretending you know what's best for me. No more blindly listening to you because you think you know better. No more sheltering me. *No.*"

Fury continued to boil out of me, winning over every other emotion.

"This whole time, I counted myself lucky to have such good friends—people who loved me in spite of our differences. But it's all been a lie."

"Lina—" This time it was Edrich's voice, soft and

gentle, and full of every imagined emotion I'd ever thought it held for me.

I shook my head and opened my eyes, glaring at him before he shut his mouth on whatever he was about to say.

"The man I look up to most in the world has a malice to him that I would've never imagined... " I turned to Uncle. "How could you do this to him? How could you do this to his father? And to me? What kind of sick person has a cure for a dying man and blackmails them before providing it?"

He tried to reach out to me, but I moved away quickly.

"And you." I said, looking up into Edrich's eyes. "How could you think I would be okay with this arrangement? That I wouldn't do everything in my power to talk Uncle into letting you out of the deal?"

Tears began to spill down my cheeks, but I didn't care that it would make him uncomfortable. "My whole life has been easier because you were my friend—" My voice cracked. "But it was a lie. Every moment of it."

I was inches away from his face at this point, trying to decipher the look of pure shock in his features.

"Lina... " Edrich whispered my name with an odd sort of reverence, and my traitorous heart fluttered in response. "Lina, you're flying."

26

EDRICH

Lina turned a brilliant, shining silver as she froze. Which, of course, meant her wings stopped working, so she started to freefall.

Wings?

I shot out a hand to catch her, still trying to wrap my head around the fact that she could *fly.* Because she had *wings.* Giant, iridescent, diaphanous wings—delicate like those of a butterfly, and nearly half as tall as she was.

When she tumbled into my hand, I felt something damp as well. Concerned, I lifted her up, twisting my hand until I could see her back. I gasped. It looked like the wings had ripped right through her skin, like they had been growing there all along and couldn't be contained any longer.

But she wasn't pulsing with pain anymore, and whatever wounds had formed when the wings popped out had already completely healed over. Either Ucafre's ointment had healed the damage as soon as it had occurred, or her body was just righting itself now that she was like she was meant to be.

Her back spasms made more sense now, though I couldn't imagine the kind of pain she had been in. The spasms that only a cream from her uncle could help...

I looked at him, my eyes narrowing.

"Did you know she would get wings?"

"You don't get to question me, boy," the troll grumbled.

Lina was angrily getting to her feet, rising to her full not-quite-five-inch height, so she could glare at Rumplestiltskin. *And me, of course.*

I had wanted to tell her the truth so many times, for so many reasons. First, just to have honesty between us, and later, because some selfish part of me wanted her to understand the way my life was tied to hers, no matter what I did. I had thought of the truth as freeing, though, somehow glossing over the part where she felt like nothing between us was real, and I was just a liar.

"Maybe he doesn't get to question you," Lina said to Rumplestiltskin, "but surely I do. The *medicine* you've been supplying me with for the last several years was supposed to *help* me? Help me what, Uncle?" She was a ball of fury. The red light glowing from her was also getting warmer by the second.

"There is so much you don't understand, Lina." Rumple looked sadder, softer than he had ever looked in my dealings with him. "I never wanted you to be in pain. But I needed to keep you safe. Keep you hidden. And those," he pointed to her wings. "Those wings tell the world who you are. That wasn't something I wanted for you."

Not for the first time, I wondered who Lina was to

him... why she was important enough for him to make deals on her behalf. *It's not my time to ask questions, though.*

"Wanted for me? What about what I wanted? What about what I needed? What right did you have to make these decisions for me?" Lina shook her head, all the shock of a moment ago giving way to a color I had never seen before, a sallow gray. If I had to go on her expression, it was somewhere between defeat and bone-deep disappointment.

Guilt clutched at my chest.

"Lina—" I started, but she shook her head, again.

She furrowed her brow in concentration, then was once again hovering in the air, her glorious wings beating softly.

"Just don't. I can't handle another lie from you, Edrich." She lifted her eyes to mine, pausing before she added. "Or another truth, for that matter." She gave the man who had been an uncle to her a last disparaging glance before she floated down to the tent opening.

"Come on, Maggie," she called, sadly. "We'll find the fairies on our own."

"You can't just leave, Lina. It's not safe," I called after her.

"Oh, right." Her tone was numb, but her voice carried from inside the tent. "I get it now, why you were always so concerned about that." She shook her head in disbelief, but she didn't get anything.

She didn't understand that the idea of her being in danger, being hurt, made me feel like I was being eaten alive by those wraiths, after all.

I didn't know how to tell her that and make her believe

it, though, so I said nothing. *Maybe she was right when she basically called me a coward earlier.*

Rumplestiltskin cleared his throat. "I know you're angry, Lina."

There was no response.

"But you can't just go off alone in this forest."

She came back out, having secured her small satchel to Maggie.

"Maggie will be with me," she said. "Besides, nothing feels quite so lonely as being with the two of you right now."

Whatever anger I felt earlier dissipated with those words, into the kind of hurt I had begun to believe I wasn't capable of feeling anymore. *Not after leaving the first time.* Even Rumplestiltskin's face broke apart.

"Even so, I won't let you be without protection."

She looked at him curiously, but with no less ire. "Do you know where the fairies are?"

That hadn't occurred to me, but his resigned expression told me he did. She took his silence as confirmation.

"Of course, you do." The words came out in a single, bitter breath. She gestured down the path. "Then, by all means. Lead the way."

27

LINA

U ncle took a step forward, his arms crossed, his face stony.

"It isn't safe—" he started, but I cut him off, my anger rising again.

"I know the forest isn't safe," I snapped, and my wings twitched in response. "But we've survived for this long, and I'm not going back to the farm."

It felt like the most natural thing in the world for the feather-light additions to be reflective of my emotions in the same way my skin was, though a quick backward glance told me only their position changed, not their color. They looked like they were made of starlight, bright and ethereal, and the hue didn't flare or fade with the intensity of my emotions.

Stranger still, they didn't feel obtrusive or foreign, more like I had been given back an essential part of me— something I didn't even realize I was missing.

But Uncle... he had known I was missing it, and now he

had the nerve to try to take yet another decision from me. I fumed, turning my attention back to him.

"You knew about them... *you knew about me!* About wherever I came from, and you kept it from me for all of these years! Did Mama know, too? Did everyone know?"

"No, child. *Ellaria* isn't safe for you," he finished.

Ellaria.

"What is Ellaria?" I asked.

Uncle stared at me unblinkingly before nodding to himself.

"Ellaria is one of the seven fairy kingdoms. It's where you're from."

Maggie nestled in next to me, and I took her comfort this time as I tried to find the lie in Uncle's words. Taking a deep breath, I tried to focus on one thing at a time.

"What do you mean it isn't safe? Why isn't it safe?" It was Edrich who voiced the question, his face twisting into concern.

But Uncle's eyes refused to leave mine as he shook his head. Then, another question bubbled from my lips.

"Did *she* know?" I didn't need to clarify who I was talking about.

"No, Lina. Your mother didn't know. I imagine she would've told you long ago if she had."

A small part of me felt relief. *Of course, she would have. I should've known better than to doubt her.*

"Well, at least there was one relationship that wasn't a lie." I squared my shoulders and ignored the flash of hurt in his eyes.

"Come on, Maggie," I said, moving forward. "It looks like we really are going to Ellaria alone, after all."

Both Edrich and Uncle were silent as we took a few

steps forward until a green hand reached out for mine. Before I could pull away, images came flooding into my vision.

No. Not images. Memories... *but they aren't mine.*

I was transported to an elaborate room, covered in vines and flowers. There was a fairy woman with teal hair and eyes and wings made of pure starlight—wings like mine—holding a baby. And wearing a crown on her head. She was crying and kissing the child over and over. Finally, she handed me the tiny girl with rosy skin and blue-green eyes. No—Not me, I realized, looking down at the scaly green arms that reached out for the child.

I was in Uncle's head. This was his memory, and I could hear his thoughts as well as my own. He had hardly ever held a baby, let alone been entrusted to protect one.

"Please. Keep her safe." The queen's voice was rich, strong, in spite of her tears.

"What if you don't come back?" he asked her.

The queen glanced over her shoulder before looking back at him, her eyes brimming with sadness.

"Then promise me you won't let her be tainted by this. By us." She wiped a tear from her cheek before her expression hardened into something more stoic. "A life for a life. You owe me." She pressed her lips to the child's head—my head—once more, and closed the windows to a large balcony where Uncle was standing.

The sounds of fighting were everywhere, and Uncle was scared. Not for himself. For the first time, he was worried for someone else. For the infant in his arms. For me. And the woman who had given her to him.

Then, the images changed.

He shushed the tiny baby me and rocked her to sleep, humming in his grating voice. If the other memory had been tinged with the dark hue of violence, this one was seen through warm, rosy tones.

The child was growing on him. A once-proud, heartless troll had somehow let this creature into his world, and she was slowly conquering it.

He hadn't heard from the Queen of Ellaria in over a month, but he had heard of the bloody war that Ellaria had lost to the western fairy kingdom of Thandria. That the entire royal family had fallen.

My chest tightened with the sadness he felt at his next thought.

He was going to have to give her up. His life wasn't suited to a child.

Then, the pictures flashed forward, and a human was there. She had long, wavy brown hair, and sparkling blue eyes. Though she was younger than I remembered her, I knew her instantly.

Mama.

She had her hands in the dirt, planting tulip bulbs, looking sadder than I had ever seen her.

"Why are you crying?" Uncle asked her, though I heard in his thoughts that he already knew the answer. He had been asking around about the kind woman for days now.

She didn't look at him with fear or disgust or disdain; the usual reactions he elicited. Only gave a small sigh, telling him the short story of how her husband had died, leaving her childless. She had no desire to remarry, but a baby—she wanted that more than anything in the world.

"Would you care if the child you had was not like the rest?"

The woman straightened her shoulders, already resembling a fiercely protective mother to a child that was only hypothetical to her.

"Of course not," she answered.

And Rumplestiltskin knew what he had to do, even if it broke whatever was left of his heart to part with the child.

"I have a solution to your problem, but it would require an oath from you to never tell anyone where she came from."

Mama considered for a moment before responding.

"As long as I have an oath from you, in return, that she was not stolen, not taken from a loving family... that she truly has no home to return to. I will not be the cause of another person's suffering."

Something in Uncle's chest eased at every sign of Mama's over-whelming goodness.

"You have my word," he said.

"Then you have mine."

The images shifted again as he passed the infant off to Mama.

There was no hesitation in her as she took the baby in a tiny walnut-shell crib—only love, joy. He promised he would check in. He would help whenever needed, but that was as much for his sake as for the woman's. He couldn't imagine not seeing how the girl grew up.

Time jumped ahead, and I saw myself hopping from flower to flower, my teal curls streaming behind me, all through Uncle's concerned gaze.

The girl could walk. She could run. She was dangerously close to being able to fly. He knew the wings would identify her as the princess who was supposed to be dead, so he searched the world for the concoction that would keep her safe, that would keep them from growing.

I felt the tears streaming down my face. I felt every emotion he felt. I saw everything he saw. Including the friendship blossoming between a young boy and the girl he called Thumbelina.

The boy was distraught. His father was dying. Uncle knew he cared for the girl, and he knew the boy was honorable. I heard the words he spoke.

"I can help your father."

The last thing I saw was a younger Edrich's hopeful expression before the vision cut off abruptly. Suddenly, I was back in the forest standing between Uncle and Edrich. I was dizzy with the amount of information he'd shared; with the years of memories that had hit all at once.

My eyes were damp and swollen, my breaths coming in fast. I didn't know what to say or think or feel. But one thing was certain now, more than ever, I knew I needed to make it to Ellaria.

Uncle seemed to read the resolve in my expression, and sighed.

"If you still want to go, I will take you myself. But we at least need to wait until morning. Please," he tacked on, and I wondered if I had ever heard him use the word before.

I found myself nodding, almost as much in shock as agreement.

"Fine," I said, emotion clogging my voice. "In the morning, then."

28

EDRICH

Though sleeping in a tent with a troll was nowhere on my bucket list, that's what I found myself doing. Well, a troll, a fairy, and her ridiculous hedgehog, but it wasn't like Lina took up much room, as tiny as she was.

Tiny.

But Rumplestiltskin had held her in his *arms* when he took her from the castle.

The sounds of their uneven breathing told me I wasn't the only one awake, but I also wasn't eager to break whatever quiet sort of truce the three of us had going. So instead, I just laid awake with a very specific memory running on repeat in my mind.

It was the day before I left our small cottage to go work with Atesh.

"Can't you just make her big?" I asked. *"Wouldn't that be the best way to keep her safe?"*

He studied me for a moment with slitted reptilian eyes, as cold and unyielding as the man they belonged to. I shivered in spite of the unnaturally warm day. I hated this man. Hated asking him for anything, but for Lina, I would risk it.

"You're concerned about her safety?"

"Isn't that what matters to you?" My cheeks reddened, sure he could see through me when I didn't quite answer.

"And I suppose she's told you she wants to be big." Something in his tone was mocking, his eyes glowing brighter with ire, though I couldn't quite figure out why.

Of course, Lina would want to be human-sized... wouldn't she?

"I haven't asked her," I admitted.

His expression morphed into something ominous, and I took several steps backward.

"I don't have anything that could make Lina big for you." He covered the distance between us and poked my chest with a bony finger. "So, I guess you'll just have to keep doing things the hard way. Protecting her, that is." He tacked on that last part with no small amount of scorn.

"No." I wasn't sure if it was a denial to what he was implying or to his statement, but I shook my head. "I'm leaving. My family is assuming my deal."

He held my gaze with his eerie one for a long moment, a moment in which I was sure he was about to tell me I couldn't go, that my father's life was forfeit the moment I left that cottage and stopped visiting Lina's farm every day.

"Then go. She doesn't need you like I thought she did. Just be sure your family holds up their end of the deal."

Trolls didn't lie. Up until now, I hadn't even been sure they *could*.

But somehow, Rumplestiltskin had lied to me back then. And I wanted to know why.

IF I HAD THOUGHT Rumplestiltskin couldn't get any more terrifying, it was only because I hadn't seen him first thing in the morning after a long night of no sleep.

Though, with a look at Lina's tangled mass of hair and the way she kept flashing red with fury at both me and her uncle, I wasn't actually sure which of them was worse right now.

I wisely kept my mouth shut for the first several hours of the journey, making noise only long enough to call Pepper back to me when she had been gone too long. Even she looked between my two companions anxiously before taking off, again.

It wasn't until we had been walking for several hours that I realized what else was off about this morning.

"The forest is quieter than it has been," I said, aloud.

So was Lina, for that matter. I wasn't sure I had ever heard her go this long without talking or humming or singing. As annoying as it had been when we took off, I would take it over this oppressive silence, any day.

After a moment of both of them ignoring me, Rumplestiltskin finally deigned to respond.

"A lot of creatures owe me favors. Didn't you wonder how I found you?" His tone was harsher than the words required, and there was an "idiot" at the end of that sentence that I was pretty sure was only unspoken for Lina's sake.

"There was a lot going on," I reminded him, edgily.

Then, we were back to saying nothing for another several hours. Only when Lina had floated far enough ahead of us that I thought she might be out of earshot was

I finally brave enough to tackle what I was really thinking about.

"You said you couldn't make her big." I muttered the accusatory words under my breath, but apparently, they weren't quiet enough.

For all her pretense of ignoring us, the fairy in question stilled slightly, her wings beating more softly than they had a moment ago, and I groaned internally. *This is likely just one more thing she's going to add to her growing list of things to hate me for.*

"Your point?" Rumplestiltskin practically hissed the words, and I came close to losing my nerve.

Then, I remembered walking away from him three years ago, and the trajectory that had followed in the wake of that conversation. Lina's hurt when she accused me of abandoning her.

"Then how was Lina the same size as you?" I challenged.

He let that hang in the air between us for a moment before responding.

"Still asking the wrong questions, I see." He walked a little faster then, making it clear he was done talking.

Lina twirled in the air, surprisingly graceful for how short a time she had been flying. But then, the wings were an extension of her. They had been there for less than a day, and already I could hardly imagine her without them.

"When did you ask him that?" Her voice was hoarse with disuse. "And why?"

I should tell her the truth, after all the lies she's already so furious about. It was hard to admit why I had wanted us to be the same size, when she so clearly despised me, though.

"I thought it would be easier for you to protect your-self that way," I said.

I swear I heard Rumplestiltskin mutter "should've been a court jester if you wanted to be a fool," under his breath, and it was an effort not to glare at the hateful little troll.

Lina just stared at me like she was willing me to under-stand, and I felt the moment she realized I still didn't. Her shoulders sagged, and she spun back around, shaking her head bitterly. I barely heard her next words. "You're the one who's blind to what's right in front of you."

I tried to ignore the way that comment felt like the wraiths had pierced me with another arrow, this one directly in my gut. It felt like she was talking about so much more than this one thing, and now was hardly the time to think about any of it.

We walked on in silence once more.

29

LINA

Hours passed until our path grew brighter. A breeze flew through my hair and wings, and I couldn't help the relief I felt as we made our way to the edge of the forest.

Warm sunlight, fresh air, and open space greeted us as we emerged from the tree line. But that wasn't all. Rolling purple hills stretched on for miles.

Ucafre was right. The hills were covered with small purple flowers that danced with the wind, just like the ripples in the lake they surrounded. It was breathtaking.

"*... Follow the river north until you pass the purple hills. That is where I last saw a fairy.*"

My heart stuttered with the realization that we were that much closer to the fairy kingdom.

That much closer to the truth about my family. My family who hadn't abandoned me at all.

I moved forward, still hovering just off the ground. My wings seemed to instinctively move on their own, as if they knew how to catch the breeze and float along it, even if my brain didn't understand it. Maggie kept pace next to me, ignoring the men behind us, or bristling and hissing at them if they came too close.

I quietly praised her each time she did it.

Every so often, I would glance back at the two people I had once trusted most in all the world. They were often just as silent as I was, but every now and then I would hear them speak. Whispered, unintelligible utterances that made me wonder what new bargain they were trying to strike without my permission.

I hated feeling this way, but there was no pulling myself out of it. So much of my life had been a lie. So many of my relationships, too. Or maybe it just felt that way, because it was true of the relationship I had cared the most about.

I squeezed my eyes shut and took a deep breath, trying to clear my head. I could either continue being hurt by the life that had been kept from me, from the realization that I had, in fact, been a burden to everyone. Or I could try to think of what would come next.

I'm a princess...

That bit of information had taken longer than the rest to sink in. *And is fairly hard to imagine it being true.*

I tried to pick it apart, dissect it, run the possibilities through my mind. If I really was this person, this princess, then I had an obligation to Ellaria, to the fairies there.

Even if I have no idea what I'm doing.

I had never felt more overwhelmed or underprepared for anything in my entire life.

I tried to think of what would come next, of how I would even greet a fairy, or try to explain who I was or where I came from—or a million other conversations that could come up, rather than the mountain of information Uncle had shared through his memories.

But one thought kept coming back to my mind again and again.

My parents didn't abandon me.

I thought back on the times I would ask him how he knew about people like me, where they were, if I would ever meet them, and his answer was always the same.

"They are long since gone, my child. There is no use trying to find them."

But they weren't. Not really. They were just on the other side of the forest...

Finally, I couldn't take it anymore and spun around, much to the surprise of everyone.

"You could have trusted me with the truth." I wasn't sure exactly which of them I was talking to.

"You mean trusted you not to run off to the fairies after I told you it was dangerous?" Uncle deadpanned.

A flush went over my skin, but I ignored it. "You had no right to make that decision for me."

"I had the right that any custodian has when they are the one caring for a child. I did what I had to do in order to keep my vow and keep you safe, and I won't apologize for that."

"You won't apologize for holding the Adler family hostage to your whims for a decade?" I seethed.

A long, uncomfortable silence followed my words. I couldn't even look at Edrich when I spoke next.

"If you ever had any love for me at all, you will release Edrich from this deal. I no longer wish for either of your protection, nor to be your burden. You owe me this much.

And you will keep providing the medicine to him, or at least allow him to purchase it."

Uncle's eyes pinched shut, but he nodded his head.

"All right, Lina," Uncle said after a moment, not bothering to glance at Edrich. "Consider it done."

I dipped my head once and looked up at Edrich. "Looks like your obligation has been met, then." I gestured around us. "We're nearly there now, then you'll never have to worry about me again."

Edrich paled, opening his mouth, then closing it again. Instead of responding to me, he looked down at Rumple. "Thank you," he said, taking a step forward.

Suddenly, Uncle's voice rang out, but not in answer. In warning.

"Don't move!" he yelled.

I flew back to investigate only to see that one of Edrich's feet was resting in a circle of mushrooms.

"What's the problem?" I asked. They looked like ordinary, white, velvety mushrooms, nothing suspicious or dangerous at all—but I knew better than to assume.

White tendrils of smoke crept out from the circle, stretching toward the three of us. Maggie whimpered and ran off into the flowers, escaping whatever poison was heading our way.

Edrich's eyes widened as he tried to escape it, though his steps were far too slow. All the while, Uncle merely shook his head and cursed under his breath. He looked me directly in the eyes before he fell to his knees, his pupils dilating and constricting again and again.

"Well," he said, his words slurred. "You got your wish. We've found the fairies. Or rather, they have found us."

30

EDRICH

Smoke billowed out of the circle of mushrooms faster than we could hope to outrun it. Lina glanced between us and the distance, like she was unwilling to fly off without us, and Rumplestiltskin was looking at her with fear in his eyes.

For her.

Was this more toxic to her, or was Lina's simply the only life he cared about?

Fear sped up my heartbeat, and for all that Lina had accused me of only caring enough to protect her because of the bargain I'd made, I knew in that moment—beyond all shadow of a doubt—just how wrong she was.

"Lina, just go!" I yelled, with the last bit of my breath, trying not to inhale the fumes.

It was no good. The smoke crept up my nostrils, and before I knew it, I was... floating. I looked down at my feet with a head that suddenly felt too light and too heavy at the same time. *Do I have wings like Lina?*

But my feet were solidly on the ground.

Something about that was funny. I laughed, and it sounded far away and distorted to my own ears. Something was niggling at me. Something decidedly not humorous.

Lina.

Lina was in danger.

It seemed to take a lifetime before I lifted my eyes up to where she had been flitting around only moments ago, but there were two more fairies there.

Or were there four?

Their shapes blurred in and out of focus, but I didn't miss that they each carried a tiny lance, or the beetle-like wings on their backs. They were brown and veiny with a thick and shiny blue shell that rested in the middle of their backs, nothing like Lina's iridescent wings. I had thought that maybe all fairies were beautiful, but these two brutes proved me wrong.

I wondered if I voiced the thought aloud, because their eyes were suddenly on me.

Or Rumple?

Moving my head around to look for the evil troll made me dizzy. Maybe he'd escaped. *Or maybe he's the green blob next to my foot.*

I blinked and looked back at the fairies, and somehow the lances they pointed at us were huge, steel tips glinting menacingly. Then another slow blink, and they were normal-sized again.

I couldn't understand what they were saying, but they seemed to be arguing. And then they were taking Lina.

"No!" I wasn't sure if I got the word out or not, but the two fairies shot vaguely distasteful looks my way while Lina's confused eyes moved between them and me and... the green blob.

No. Rumplestiltskin.

He was laughing, too, or something like it, the sound like a heavy iron chain grating against itself. The colors around us were shifting like Lina's skin, coming into focus sharply and then fading into a fuzzy, scattered landscape.

I couldn't tell how long I spent wondering at the kaleidoscope around me before I looked around again to find that Lina was gone.

Distantly, I registered that the thought should cause me some panic, but I was distracted by the curious sensation of my limbs becoming painfully tight, the world around me shrinking and expanding.

They found us, Rumplestiltskin had said. If this was what Ellaria did to unsuspecting strangers, I wondered if Lina had any real idea what she was getting herself into.

31

LINA

P anic swelled in my chest.

What is happening?

The two fairies put down their weapons as soon as Edrich and Uncle were dazed and giggling, clearly deeming me as unthreatening, then they began arguing with each other in hushed tones. Every so often, they would look at me and then their arguing would continue again.

They wore leather armor that accommodated wings which looked as if they'd been plucked straight from a giant beetle. Once I saw my own wings, I had imagined that all fairies might look the same, but I was fascinated by how much variation there could be.

As much as I was excited to see fairies, actual fairies, I was also terrified and furious. Heat bloomed under my skin and I could see the ruby halo glowing around me. Just because Edrich's feelings had been forced didn't mean I could shut mine off so easily.

I can't lose him.

Either of them, I amended, looking back at where

Edrich and Uncle Stiltskin were still giggling softly to themselves.

"What did you do to them?" I asked the flying men above me, my voice louder than I meant it to be.

I replayed the moment Edrich stepped on the mushrooms in my mind again and again, and I couldn't help wondering why they had only affected him and Uncle or how long the effects would last.

"Just a bit of pixie dust." One of the fairies gave a wicked sort of smile, the expression at odds with his soft sapphire hair and crystalline eyes.

"Don't be cryptic, Gentian." The other one with the emerald hair, bronze skin, and honey-colored eyes shook his head disapprovingly. "It's just the mushroom's natural gas, or spores, not something we did."

"Will they be all right?" I asked, incredulously.

"The confusion will wear off in a couple of hours," the one named Gentian said. His slightly ominous expression didn't change, and it didn't escape my notice that he hadn't directly answered my question.

I turned my gaze to the other one. He looked between me and his fellow guard with an unreadable expression.

"The gas doesn't hurt them, and this valley is a place of peace." He met my eyes steadily, and I was inclined to believe him.

I was still reluctant to leave, and I realized it wasn't because I doubted their safety, not really. Everything we had come across was terrified by just the idea of Uncle, and Edrich could take care of himself.

If I was being honest with myself, I knew Uncle would find a way to see me again. But Edrich... *Am I ready to walk away from him like this?*

Would he be relieved when he came to his senses and realized he didn't have to worry about me anymore?

While I was lost in my thoughts, the two fairies had been staring at my new wings. Uncle's words about how the wings would make me recognizable came flooding back to me.

"It's her, Oren. There's no mistaking it. Look at her," Gentian said.

My red glow faded, and I felt something else seeping in and muting the angry color. A soft, pale yellow. *Hope.*

"I know. Only a fool wouldn't recognize her." Oren sighed, running a hand through his emerald hair. "We need to take her directly to the Queen."

My heart dropped to the pit of my stomach. *The Queen?*

Maybe it was naive of me, but I couldn't help but hope that Uncle had lied, or at the very least, that he had been mistaken. That maybe this queen was... my mother. My real mother. *Maybe I still have a family, after all.*

"No," Gentian argued. "All of Ellaria deserves to know about her first."

My heart continued to hammer within my chest with the possibility of meeting the woman I'd seen in Uncle's memories.

"There is no sense in raising undue alarm," Oren responded, quietly.

"Did you intend to ask if I wanted to come with you, or were you planning to force me?" I spat out.

Their full attention was on me. I swallowed hard, feeling completely unprepared for whatever would happen next.

"Forgive us, My Lady. My name is Oren, and this is Gentian." The one with green hair told me what I had

174 ELLE MADISON & ROBIN D. MAHLE

already guessed. "We assumed you had come in search of Ellaria, and as sentries for the Kingdom, we would be honored to escort you there."

I felt dizzy. This was all happening so fast. And none of it was going according to plan.

And then there was Maggie. Tears pricked at my eyes as I thought of my best friend. She had taken off in the commotion, and while I knew she would find her way back here, that was another goodbye that I hadn't planned on giving. I had expected that she would be with me until the end, and that we would do this together.

I darted a glance around the field, flying higher to see if I could make out her form scurrying through the flowers.

"But, my hedgehog—" I started, emotion choking my voice.

The two men looked at each other, puzzled, until Gentian spoke up.

"We need to return before night closes in, if we expect to make it within the gates before dawn."

"I'm sorry," Oren added. "But he's right.

I looked around, again, thinking maybe she would come back, maybe I would get to say goodbye or convince them to let me bring her. But I knew that wasn't likely. *And haven't I come all this way to see Ellaria? To find answers?*

After a moment, I nodded, and Oren smiled.

And maybe it was because I couldn't imagine having come all this way, of being this close, and not finding out the truth of where I came from or who I was.

Or maybe it was the million questions running wild through my mind, or the fact that sticking around and actually saying goodbye to the three most important beings in my life would probably break me that made me do it.

Either way, I had come too far to go back now.

Besides, I was just being dramatic. It's not like I would be trapped there forever. I could go back to the farm if I wanted, or I could send word later.

The next thing I knew, I was placing my hand in Oren's —he was clearly the more trustworthy of the two—and flying toward a home I had no memory of.

It was all I could do to hope this wasn't the biggest mistake of my life.

❦ 32 ❧

EDRICH

My vision gradually became clearer, but my reality
still seemed to be wrong. Everything was dark,
and panic was slowly ebbing in—so cloying it felt like a
centaur was sitting on my chest. I struggled to catch my
breath, and that's when I realized it wasn't just panic.

There actually is something crushing me.

My eyes popped open, and all I could make out was a
small shaft of light coming through what looked like a tent
seam. *But I hadn't made camp tonight.* There shouldn't be a
tent, certainly not one as heavy as this that seemed to be
supported by nothing.

I willed myself not to give in to this claustrophobic
feeling, taking air in slowly. *There.* I could breathe and
focus enough to realize that the fabric wasn't actually
heavy enough to restrict my movements.

I squirmed around a bit to get a better vantage point
on the light, until I could see that it wasn't only a seam,
but what looked like... a buttonhole. And what was making

the fabric feel so heavy was a giant wooden button, nearly the size of my entire head.

Who makes a tent with a giant button and no sticks?

More importantly, why am I in here alone? And where is Lina?

I racked my brain furiously, trying to remember as much as I could of what happened before everything went fuzzy. We had been walking through the valley, and I stepped into a mushroom circle. Rumplestiltskin had looked afraid—for Lina.

And she...

She had left with the fairies.

Of her own free will? Or forcibly? I strained to remember what felt like a dream. She'd looked back sadly. Her mouth moved, but I hadn't heard what she'd said. Then, she flew after the two fairies.

"Rumplestiltskin?" Maybe the goblin was still here. *Or maybe he's gone after her.*

I bolted up to better access the button in an effort to escape, to go after her, wherever that was... and that's when I noticed something else, something nearly as important as the fact that someone had buttoned me into this weird cocoon.

I was naked.

What in sweet fairy hell is going on?

I managed to undo the button, with no small amount of aggravation, finally stepping into the hazy, overcast light of the world outside. My eyes were still adjusting when a gruff voice startled me.

"For the love of the forsaken forest," Rumplestiltskin grumbled. "Put these on." A wad of fabric hit me before I saw it coming, and I felt my cheeks warm.

These weren't my clothes, wherever they had gone, but I scrambled into the soft tunic and leggings he had thrown at me, before I finally looked around.

My jaw dropped.

Rumplestiltskin had grown, somehow. Not stretched out, but proportionally, so he was nearly my height now but twice as wide. His scowl was even more horrifying up close, his pupils a swirling mass of gold and onyx instead of the solid color they had appeared before.

"How are you big?" I blurted out.

If anything, his scowl deepened.

"The girl was too easy on you," he muttered. "Not so much blind as stupid, are you?"

I looked skyward before I said something that would only make us both angrier, when we needed to focus on finding Lina... but what I saw stopped me short. I had been so fixated on him, so caught up in the oddity of the situation, I hadn't bothered to look around me.

At first, I thought we were no longer in the valley, but in a strange, purple forest. Then, my gaze landed on the fabric beneath me, a very specific shade of blue, one Lina had told me years ago was her favorite color for me to wear.

Rumplestiltskin was right. *I am stupid.*

I was standing on my shirt—my shirt which I was no longer wearing, because it was far, far too big for me. And the purple forest... it was the violets, only they were taller than I was.

Because I was the size of a fairy. And so was Rumplestiltskin.

"This is how you were holding her." I finally spoke after staring around in disbelief for what felt like an hour, but was probably more like five minutes. "She wasn't big. You... you were tiny."

"Nothing gets by you." He rolled his eerie yellow eyes.

I can't even fault him, this time.

"We have to go after her," I said, abruptly. "You said you knew where the fairy kingdom is."

"Of course, we'll go after her," he grumbled, muttering something that sounded suspiciously like "useful as dragon fodder" under his breath. "But what took her a couple of hours by flight, will take us days on the ground."

"We don't have days." I shook my head.

"We don't have a choice," he grated. "It's safe to say you aren't hiding any wings under there, given that I just saw more of you than anyone would ever want to."

I scowled at him, but it did beg the question...

"Do you often travel with fairy-sized clothes?"

He shot me a look that was half-disgust and half-condescending.

"This isn't my first trip to Ellaria, and since I was going with the village idiot, I figured you might activate the mushrooms."

I couldn't decide if it was more or less offensive that he had been right, so I ignored him, focusing instead on the intricate details of the world around me—things I had never noticed before. Like the thick lines running up and down each blade of grass, or how many tiny pieces of thread went into the main line that carefully stitched my black leather boots—boots that were now several inches taller than I was.

And moving.

I jerked backward a step, my hand going to a sword that was no longer there. *Perfect.* I was small and unarmed, and one of my giant boots was moving. And... grunting? Before I had time to panic, a pointy brown snout came poking around the side of my boot, followed by a quill-covered head.

A giant hedgehog.

Or, rather, a normal-sized hedgehog, next to a minia-ture-sized me—something I still couldn't wrap my brain around.

"Maggie?" I wasn't sure why I phrased it as a question, when I was fairly certain no one else was going around randomly painting hedgehog toenails and fitting them with makeshift saddles.

Makeshift saddles...

I exchanged a resigned look with Rumplestiltskin.

Never in a million years did I think a saddled hedgehog would be useful, but I wasn't going to look a gift-hog in the mouth. *At least now we have a faster way to get to Lina.*

33

LINA

We flew until the sun began to set, heading straight for the tree line on the other side of the meadow. The two fairies guiding me didn't spare me more than a few backward glances for most of the journey. They remained silent except for the whispers of frustration they had for each other. So, for hours, I had nothing to do but think, which was dangerous.

From the way that they hadn't threatened me or forced me to come with them, I felt relatively safe. However, there was still something they weren't saying, and they made little effort to speak to me.

I reminded myself that the dangerous beings of the forest had stayed clear of us since Uncle had shown up. That even though they were delirious when we'd left them, I felt relatively certain that as long as Edrich stayed with him, they'd be safe.

If not from each other, then at least from everything else.

I glanced back in the direction we'd come from, but there was no sign of any of them. And we hadn't seen any creatures in the meadow aside from a few woodland animals. It seemed peaceful, especially in comparison to the forest we'd trekked through to reach it.

Surely if this place was dangerous, the animals wouldn't feel so at ease.

Fireflies began to twinkle as the sun dipped lower on the horizon. They had seemed to be lighting the way for the three of us as we flew toward a wall of twisted and knotted trees.

I shivered from the evening's dropping temperature. I hadn't been wearing more than my thin sleeveless dress when Maggie had taken off. It was one of the few things that had accommodated my new wings. Crossing my arms, I ran my hands over them quickly, trying to infuse some warmth into myself.

The men must've noticed, because they slowed their pace and flew a little closer. The heat emanating from them seemed to stifle the chill, but only slightly.

"We're almost there," Gentian offered, with a small smile of reassurance.

Oren sighed.

"This is a mistake," he muttered, under his breath.

I looked at the emerald-haired fairy, and though his tone was tense, there seemed to be something more than irritation in his eyes.

Fear?

I didn't have much time to guess at what it was before we were finally coming to a stop at the base of the tree wall.

It was even more complex up close. The trees had indeed grown together, twisting in a way that fused each trunk and branch to the one next to it. Vines and leaves filled any empty space, making up one of the most impressive and beautiful walls I'd ever seen.

"This way, My Lady," Gentian offered.

We walked forward, and a small opening appeared at the base of one of the tree trunks.

No, not just an opening. A door.

Oren led me through, while Gentian took up the rear, either following us in or making sure I wasn't thinking of a last-minute escape, I couldn't be sure.

Once we were through the door, I gasped, spinning in a slow circle to take everything in.

It's an entire world built for people like me.

A smile stretched wide over my mouth while I noticed wagons and gardens and rivers. Houses were built from thick mushrooms or foliage. Music poured from shops and taverns designed in much the same way.

Squirrels and hedgehogs and mice pulled wagons with wares, while fairies flooded the streets, minding their business, perfectly oblivious that any other world existed beyond this one.

And why shouldn't they?

"This is extraordinary," I whispered, still awestruck.

My escorts looked at each other with some unspoken expression and shrugged.

"This is the *common* sector for—" Gentian began incredulously, but Oren cut him off.

"He means the working sector," he clarified. "This is where all of Ellaria gets their food, and where the more humble work is done."

Gentian muttered something about menial work, and Oren nudged him in the side. It may be humble to them, but to me, it was everything I'd ever dreamed of. A world I could live in, filled with people like me.

I cursed myself for wishing that somehow Edrich had been able to see this with me. I knew he would be just as awestruck as I was. *Or maybe he wouldn't...*

I stumbled over the ridiculous thought. He wouldn't have even been able to squeeze through the trees... or walk through the door the way we had.

And then again, he was probably grateful he wasn't here—that I was no longer his burden.

"Wait until you see the castle," Oren whispered, interrupting me from my thoughts as he pointed up toward the canopy.

Suddenly, I felt dizzy. I had been so fixated on everything down on the ground that I hadn't even noticed the sprawling lights and buildings carved into the trees above. The whole thing looked like a spiral climbing toward the sky, each level grander and more ornate than the one below it.

In the center was a great tree, wider than the rest in the tree wall surrounding it. It climbed high above us and, near the top, there were mushrooms and braided branches with vines and flowers all surrounding one great structure.

I looked back down at the ground to steady myself as a few fairies passed us on the street and stopped to stare, first at my escorts, then at me. Their shock was clear as they took in the three of us, but what seemed to hold their attention most were the wings on my back.

Another thought struck me, practically knocking the wind from my lungs—the knowledge that every single one of these people might have known my family. My real family.

And that I am supposedly their princess.

I still hadn't wrapped my head around that yet. *I'm not sure if I am even capable of it.*

There must have been nearly a hundred fairies crowding around and staring at us, most of them bowing as we moved past them. I didn't miss the way they quickly turned their heads to not meet my eyes when I would glance back.

"Do you see her wings?"

"No mistaking her... "

"Queen Hyacinth's daughter."

"Where has she been all these years?"

"What will Queen Cassia do?"

The last question ripped every last vestige of hope from me. If I was Hyacinth's daughter, then Cassia must be from the kingdom that overthrew my family.

A tremor of fear raked up my spine.

The men who'd brought me here had been kind enough, but under the intense stares of everyone else, I began to wonder why Uncle felt this place wasn't safe for me. What it meant to be recognized as their dead princess.

I felt myself shifting from one color to the next in quick succession.

There were a few gasps at that, and my escorts nearly blushed when they caught sight of my ever-changing emotional state.

"Happy now? Everyone has seen her, or will hear about her presence soon enough. We need to get her to the castle," Oren warned Gentian, who only nodded.

Both men looked at me and then up toward the glowing lights above.

"It's time," Oren said, his voice softer.

Without another word, each man took one of my hands, and we slowly flew upward. More fairies emerged from the windows of the buildings or homes carved into the trees, or nests on the branches, all to catch sight of us. All of them wore the same expression of shock, and even fear, when their eyes landed on me.

With every tier we flew past, dread pooled in my stomach. Some of them darted past us, heading toward our destination before we could. Oren cursed under his breath, but didn't increase his speed. Gentian fidgeted nervously, as more and more gathered above us.

When we finally came to a stop near the top of the great tree, we landed on a wide plateau of branches, braided and covered in moss and flowers with a walkway to the grandest structure I'd ever seen.

There was no mistaking that this was a castle. *The* castle.

Ornate balconies, windows, and doors were carved into the tree trunk. Mushrooms, moss, and flowers grew over the structure making up the siding. Small lanterns hung on either side of the entrance, with the same glowing moss from the forest lighting them.

In my wildest dreams, I would never have imagined anything like it. It seemed happy. Enchanting. Something plucked from the sweet dreams of a child.

Most surprising of all was that the woman who walked through the doors was no different. I had expected her to be a monster, knowing what she might have done to my family, but instead she matched the castle behind her.

Every fairy nearby bowed to the regal-looking woman with a golden circlet woven into her cinnamon hair.

Almond-colored eyes matched the wings behind her that dipped nearly to the ground, and she wore a gown made of rose petals and ivy.

But it wasn't her eyes or her gown or her wings that unnerved me. It was the cautiously clinical way she assessed me, as if... as if I was the dangerous one.

✣ 34 ✣

EDRICH

Riding Maggie across the valley may have been the faster solution, but it certainly wasn't the most comfortable. My arm ached from holding it in front of me to fend off the weeds and stems whipping into my face with each flitting step. If I sat forward too far, Maggie would get irritated and raise her quills just enough to scrape my arms.

And that's not even the worst of it.

"You're leaning again," a grouchy voice said into my ear.

That was the worst of it. The scaly troll sitting at my back and griping into my ear every three seconds.

"Well, you insisted on sitting back there," I reminded him, for the thousandth time in the hours since we had taken off.

Whatever he was going to say was cut off as we both ducked to avoid a bumblebee zooming toward us. It didn't seem to intend us any harm, but that didn't stop my heartbeat from thundering in my chest as it flew by, buzzing so loudly that I nearly had to cover my ears.

When you were this size, something didn't necessarily need to mean you harm to inflict it, and that thing's stinger had been the size of my arm.

Well, practically.

I was torn somewhere between wondering where Pepper was and being glad she hadn't swooped in to eat me. *Here's to hoping she recognizes me if she does find me...*

The ride also left far too much time for me and my thoughts. Lina had insisted that Rumplestiltskin free me, and whether or not he wanted to, he couldn't go back on his word.

I was relieved for my father's sake, but I didn't feel any less burdened like I expected to. If anything, losing that last tether to Lina only made me feel... empty.

Leaving the medallion behind, on the other hand, had been surprisingly easy. For all that it hadn't left my neck in three years, the past few months had made wearing it feel more like a shackle than a privilege.

As much as I wanted to get to Lina, my frazzled nerves were ready for a break when we finally stopped for the night. At least we had a tent and a reasonably comfortable place to sleep. Rumplestiltskin had pulled an entire fairy-sized pack out of his normal one for this journey, and Maggie still had some of Lina's supplies in her saddlebag.

I tried not to think about her as I rifled through them, the way she left without so much as a goodbye. She had told us she would leave once she found the fairies... but part of me never really believed she would.

I told myself that as long as she was safe, I would leave again, let her be happy with her own people, just as my mother had said years ago. That didn't stop the sinking feeling when I pulled out her bedroll, trying to ignore the way it held her scent of fresh flowers and sunshine.

How was it so easy for her to walk away? Because she didn't care? Or, more likely. *Because she thought I didn't?*

I was unrolling the bedroll next to Rumple's in our tent, which was little more than twigs and canvas, when something started moving underneath the fabric. I jumped back, pulling the bedroll with me until I saw it, an enormous brown cylinder burrowing from the ground beneath.

"Snake!" I called to Rumplestiltskin, grasping once again for a weapon that wasn't there.

The green man looked over irritably, not a trace of surprise or fear on his features.

"Earthworm," he corrected, shaking his head at my idiocy. "Just leave it be and it'll go away."

Sure enough, a second look at the slimy, cone-shaped head proved him right. It squirmed around aimlessly for a moment before Maggie darted over and ripped it from the ground. She chomped away on it, and the sound churned my stomach. Either I hadn't noticed how loud and squelchy her eating habits were, or my hearing was more sensitive now. Either way, it made my stomach uneasy.

Something rustled outside of the tent, and I startled, again.

"Just a weed hitting the tent. Go to sleep," Rumple growled.

I let loose a stilted breath, cursing myself for the uncharacteristic jumpiness.

"How does she live like this?" I didn't realize I had asked the question aloud, until Rumplestiltskin actually chuckled under his breath.

"She doesn't. Lina knows the difference between a snake and an earthworm just fine."

"You know what I mean." I shot him an irritable look. "How has she even survived in a world where literally everything can kill her?"

"You mean like that worm?" He raised his eyebrows.

I just waited him out.

"Fairies are different than humans," he reluctantly explained, passing me a pecan as long as my forearm. I took a bite while he kept talking. "They give off a scent to would-be predators letting them know they aren't prey, aren't enemies. That's not to say that an animal can't strike before realizing that, but as long as a fairy is reasonably careful, they have little to worry about from the animal world. Most things are just curious about them."

All those times Lina had said something was just coming to say hello and I had accused her of being naive, she had been right.

"You must give off the opposite scent." I thought of the way everything in the forest seemed to shy away from him.

"When I'm full-sized, yes. It does seem to be diminished in this form." He glanced at where Maggie was still munching on the earthworm.

Well, that's just fantastic.

I finished eating wordlessly, and Maggie came over, sniffing at Lina's pack.

Right.

I opened it up and unfolded the blanket I'd seen her sleep in before. She snatched it from my hands with her teeth and rolled until it was snugly wrapped around her just outside of our tent.

Even before I settled in my bedroll, I could tell it was going to be a long night.

It wasn't only my murky thoughts keeping me awake, either. Everything was so *loud*. The wind whistled through the grass, each blade creating its own high-pitched tune. A creepy shuffling sound outside our tent made me pop my head out, and then immediately back in, when I beheld a spider half as tall as I was rubbing its hairy legs against one another.

I sat inside the tent, squeezing the flaps closed and hoping that every one of its eight eyes was fixated somewhere other than my stupid, curious head. After a few minutes passed, I finally breathed a sigh of relief, laying back against my makeshift pillow.

Just as I lost all hope of falling asleep, another sound reached my ears. But this one was... enchanting.

It began as a simple, melodic strain, then was joined in by different pitches and tones all around the tent, creating a symphony that was in perfect unison. Crickets, I finally realized. But what sounded like chirping to my larger, human ears, was an orchestra now, each part distinct and a perfect complement to the others.

For all the dangers of Lina's world, there was beauty there, too. Maybe that was how she stayed so much happier than the rest of us did, because of these everyday joys that only she could see and appreciate.

A pang went through me at the thought that I might never be able to tell her that—might never be able to explain that I finally saw how narrow-minded I had been all these years. Then, the symphony picked back up, and somehow, inexplicably, it lulled me into sleep.

🦋 35 🦋

LINA

Oren and Gentian cleared their throats and signaled that I should bow, as well. I felt my pulse in my temples as I attempted to copy the motion of everyone around me.

I did my best, having never bowed before anyone before, and nearly lost my balance in the process. Piper was the only princess I knew, but she was so informal and unlike any stories of other royals I'd ever heard of.

In fact, she probably would have laughed if I'd tried to curtsy or bow before her.

As I shifted to stand, I caught the queen's eyes. Again, they were assessing me, but this time there was the smallest hint of what might have been confusion there, also. I was frustrated, again, to realize I was the only one of my people who seemed to change colors with my emotions.

This situation would be a lot easier to read, otherwise.

I stood to face the queen, my voice catching in my

throat. Her gaze finally left my eyes to linger on the massive wings behind me.

"Ixia," she spoke at last, her voice as warm as the auburn tones of her hair. "You're alive."

I looked around for some sign of who she might be speaking to before it dawned on me. *Of course,* Uncle would hardly have kept my name if he wanted to keep me hidden.

Once again, I had to wonder why he went to such great lengths to keep me away.

I blushed bright pink all over my body when I realized I had trailed off in my thoughts again and left everyone waiting.

The queen widened her eyes at the sight of my mood-changing skin tone. Another sign that there weren't many things about me that were normal.

"It's Lina, actually." I finally found my voice to respond to the name she gave me. *Ixia.*

The queen merely held my gaze for a prolonged moment before giving the barest tilt of her chin. "If you say so." Then, she turned to the guards, a question in her exquisite features.

"Queen Cassia." Oren dipped his head. "We found her traveling through the Amethyst Ridge."

"All alone?" She turned back to me for that question.

"No." There was no point in lying when the guards had seen us. "My companions traveled with me until I met Oren and Gentian, who were kind enough to escort me here."

"And what of your companions?" she asked, expression carefully neutral.

"Gentian assured me they would be safe in the valley," I

responded, trying not to look down at my feet in guilt. "And we had always planned to part ways once I found my way here." I stumbled over that last word.

I didn't want to think about that moment when I had turned my back on Edrich and walked away from our pretense of friendship forever—didn't want to think about how much that decision had made me feel like my heart was physically breaking into a thousand pieces.

The queen's brow twitched, infinitesimally, and the fairies behind me stiffened.

"The valley is fairly safe, yes, but we will send others out to ensure their safety, as well." She said this in a cool, insistent voice that brooked no arguments.

"Thank you," I responded, uncertainly, not at all sure that her offer was sincere.

The queen only took in my pallid green color for a moment before she nodded, turning back toward the castle in a single, fluid motion. She signaled for me to follow her, and I held my breath as the castle doors closed behind us.

It felt momentous, if not a little ominous.

"You say you go by Lina?" she asked, as she led me down a corridor lined with more guards who stood straighter as we passed.

"Yes, that's what my mother called me," I told her.

This time, I was not mistaking the fear that flickered through her eyes.

"The woman who birthed you?" she clarified, in a quiet voice.

"No," I answered, slightly on the defensive. "My mama, the woman who raised me."

Her lips parted, a small whoosh of air escaping them. My skin glowed a confused sort of teal at her relief.

"Not a fairy, I presume." The corner of her lips tilted up as we rounded a corner and headed for a grand staircase. We began climbing the steps before I answered her.

"No, a human."

Does she find that lacking? Her expression had gone blank again, and she only nodded like that was the answer she was expecting.

After leading me to a large door, she gestured, and the guards in the hall were quick to open it. We walked through, and the sound of the door closing shut behind us seemed to echo off the walls.

Surely, she wouldn't bother to walk me to this room just to kill me, especially after she greeted me in front of all those people. In spite of the things she was supposed to have done, she didn't quite seem evil.

"Why did you come back?" She broke the silence, abruptly.

I stopped in my tracks. Just this morning, I had thought I knew exactly why I was coming here. Now, the answer didn't seem so clear.

"I wanted to find others like me." *I didn't want to be alone, but somehow, I still feel that way even surrounded by my own kind.*

She fixed me with another of her coolly assessing glances before speaking again.

"Do you remember your birth mother at all?" she asked.

The room was dark with a few rays of the setting sun peeking in through the windows. Flowers and vines covered the walls, making it feel as if we were back in the forest... or the meadow. I turned in a slow circle to take in the rest of the room, in awe of its utter perfection.

There was a massive wooden bed on one side, with a gauzy cream-colored canopy hanging above it, and a seating area on the other side. Every piece of furniture was made to fit someone my size. Each hand-carved or painted item practically took my breath away.

How long have I dreamed of a room that was just for me?

The queen cleared her throat, and I realized the time that passed since she asked her question.

Centaurs.

She repeated her question, more tensely this time.

"No," I answered honestly, and she seemed to relax. "But I know that she was Queen of Ellaria."

"She was." She seemed to be waiting for me to go on.

"I know that she sent me away, because she feared for my life." I forced myself to meet her eyes before I said the next part. "Because of you?"

The queen squeezed her eyes shut, then opened them again. "I imagine so."

"Did she... did she have a reason to?"

"I suppose that depends on who you ask," she said, with an unexpected gentleness.

"And what about now?" I barely got the words out.

"There is much you do not understand, Ix—Lina," she said. "I know that you have no reason to believe me when I tell you that you have nothing to fear from me."

I wanted to accept that, but... "Did you kill my parents?"

Her entire body stilled, but her gaze was steady when it met mine.

"It is much more complex than that, and there may

well be pieces of it that you will wish you hadn't heard, things that will tarnish the way you see those you would prefer to hold dear." She raised a hand when she saw my protesting expression. "I am not unwilling to tell you, but it is not a story I will impart tonight."

Her expression softened.

"You need rest, Little One. And time, I believe, to process. There will be plenty enough tomorrow, if you insist on hearing it, but just remember that a truth given, cannot be taken back." She smiled sadly before sweeping gracefully into the hallway, leaving me there with only my churning thoughts for company.

✵ 36 ✵

EDRICH

For all that I had appreciated the wonders of the world around me last night, the dangers were even more apparent by the light of day. From atop Maggie, I could spy all manner of activity going on around me, and there was something to be cautious of in each of them.

Fire ants marched in perfect order, and all I could think was that a bite from them could set half my leg searing with the size I was now. Dragonflies flitted by, their wingspan longer than I was, and even the field mice could probably have bitten me in half, if they wanted to.

This peaceful valley managed to feel infinitely more dangerous than the forest had, unarmed and off-kilter as I was in this new, unfamiliar size.

I was so focused on all the remote possibilities of danger that I nearly missed the reality of it, even when Maggie balked a bit, shuffling away from the direction we had been headed. When Rumple looked sharply around, and the grass near us began to rustle, I finally looked to my left.

I had just enough time to reflect on how ridiculous it had been of me to call the earthworm from the night before a snake. There was no mistaking the thing looming before me, jaws opened at an impossible angle to reveal razor-sharp fangs as tall as my hand.

A fairly common valley snake, one I never would have had to worry about as an adult human, but it could kill me now. Maggie tried to run, her quills standing on end and pricking at my legs. It wasn't long before she curled up into herself, throwing Rumple and me to the ground.

I barely had time to register the fall before the snake slithered closer, its speed otherworldly. And from the way it was reared back, poised for a strike. There was no way to tell who it was aiming for, and no time to dodge. I only had time enough for a single thought.

One of us is going to die.

The snake lunged forward, its fangs longer than my torso, and sharp as steel. Just before it could end our lives, the four of us were startled by a *kakking* sound, one so much louder and richer and more ominous in this form—but familiar, nonetheless.

Pepper.

My gyrfalcon shot in with an unparalleled speed and grace, gripping the snake in her claws and knocking us over with the intensity of the wind from her wings.

Once the snake was in her grasp, she soared up into the sky with it until I lost sight of her. Rumple and I risked a glance at one another, both of us speechless as we contemplated how close we came to death.

"How did you survive being this size before?" I asked, panting, as Maggie came over to rest her snout on my leg.

"By having the basic amount of sense afforded most

intelligent creatures, and not travelling with people who didn't." He practically spat the words at me, but I didn't miss the way his breaths were coming in too fast, or the panic in his eyes.

He is just as scared as I am.

"Feel free to offer some better advice then, for how to get to Lina," I shot back. "I am very open to suggestions."

He rolled his eyes and stood to brush the dirt off his knees, while I picked up the few items of Lina's that had fallen from Maggie's pack.

A hedgehog was definitely not the most suitable steed, given that she could turn into a ball of sharp spines when it suited her. I was glad she was safe, though. An attack like that with Hobgoblin could have been the end of him.

Another several minutes passed before Pepper swept back down, coming to an abrupt stop right in front of us.

Pepper tipped her head, examining me. For a moment, I thought she might try to eat me, but she only gently moved forward until her beak was within arm's length. I put a hesitant hand out, stroking the tiny feathers above her beak, and she fluffed her wings contentedly.

Thank the fairies, she recognizes me.

She caught sight or whiff of Rumplestiltskin, though, and hopped several paces backward, fixing him with her predator's stare.

"I guess whatever you're exuding isn't too diminished." I raised my eyebrows at the small green man.

He only shrugged.

"Maggie must just be used to me."

I looked between Maggie and Pepper, an idea forming in my mind. Just as I opened my mouth to speak, Rumplestiltskin cut in.

"You don't know the first thing about Ellaria, Boy."

My thoughts must have been written on my face.

"But I know a thing or two about recon," I shot back. "And besides, we need to get to her quickly if there is even a chance she's in danger. I doubt Pepper will consent to carry you." I brushed aside any trepidation I had at being held in the falcon's talons... or tumbling from her back mid-air.

"I knew you were stupid," he said, like he could read my thoughts. "But you can't honestly tell me you expect to ride a bird without so much as a saddle?"

"I'll do whatever I have to do, to get to her," I told him, earnestly.

He looked at me for a moment, his usual scorn absent from his reptilian features. Then, he blinked, something like guilt replacing his assessing glance. "I didn't have a chance to tell her everything before she left."

I blinked. "You mean, there's more than the whole, *your parents didn't abandon you and you're actually the princess of a race most people don't even think exists*, thing?" I was half joking, but the serious expression on his face stopped me short.

Whatever he wasn't saying, I could see in his swirling black eyes that he thought it would be the truth to break her.

LINA

Gentle sunlight pulled me from the few hours of reluctant, fitful sleep I had managed to wrangle. The bed was beyond comfortable, but being alone with my thoughts for the first time in days wasn't as peaceful as I might have hoped.

I told myself that was the only reason, not because I missed Edrich's even breaths beside me, or his stoic, comforting presence. Certainly not after I had been humiliated when nothing turned out to be what I thought it was.

I tried to wrap my brain around that. A lifetime worth of friendship... could he possibly have been faking all of it? *Does it even matter now?* It's not like we would be in each other's lives anymore, not if I made my life here. *If that is even an option.*

A light knock on the door interrupted my latest maelstrom of thoughts.

"Come in." I sat up in time for the queen to enter, carrying a silver filigree tray, laden with food.

I couldn't get over the way everything here was the right size. I was so accustomed to drinking out of larger cups and taking small bites of huge portions of food. On her tray was a porcelain teacup small enough for me to lift with one hand, and a croissant I could eat without making a flaky mess.

My stomach growled at the scent of perfectly portioned sausage, and the queen gave me a tentative smile.

"I thought you might be hungry."

"Starving," I admitted.

"And, if you would like... " Her smile faltered. "While you eat, I will tell you what transpired all those years ago."

I had thought about this last night, weighed the pain of knowing against the frustration of living in ignorance. *Again.* So I was ready for her question—ready to nod my assent.

"I would appreciate that very much," I told her, truthfully.

She set the tray down in front of me, and I made myself a plate while she settled into a green velvet armchair.

"My husband was born the second son to the king of Thandria. Things are different there. It was not so strange for him to find his bride among commoners." She gestured to herself with a half-smile. "To marry for love rather than position. We were happy there, for a time."

I couldn't quite see where my family, my kingdom, fit into any of this yet... but something in her tone told me that, maybe, I didn't want to know. Still, I didn't stop her.

"Not long after our first child was born, there was an attack on our people, from a kingdom north of us." She looked cautiously over to where I had frozen with my teacup halfway to my lips. "One known for its brutality. There were devastating losses." Her voice cracked on that last word.

"So we joined together with a kingdom from the far east to ensure it would never happen to anyone again. Because of the loss we had suffered at their hands, it was decided that my husband and I would rule the conquered kingdom." She paused then, waiting for me to put the pieces together.

So I did, even though every part of me rebelled at the idea.

"The kingdom that attacked you was Ellaria," I said hoarsely.

"Yes."

I tried to reconcile what she was saying against the memory Rumplestiltskin had shown me.

"Then why was my mother afraid for my life?"

My door opened abruptly, and a girl around my age sauntered in.

"Because killing you in retaliation is what she would have done," the girl said casually, holding out her hand to reveal a small, frosted pastry. "A cupcake for the usurper?"

"Aster! Eavesdropping is not ladylike." The queen shook her head. "And honestly... show a little decorum."

I stretched out my hand numbly to take her offered dessert, but I hardly processed the rest, because my mind snagged on one word. Retaliation. What had the queen said? *The loss they suffered.*

"Your child?" I managed to croak out.

"Was killed in the attack."

"By my parents?" I asked.

"By their soldiers," she said, gently. *Gently*, as if even now, she was trying to shield me from the truth—from the reason the people had cowered in fear when I arrived.

My parents had been monsters.

Cassia took note of my expression and rested a hand on my arm. "All these years, I have wondered if because of me, another child was a casualty of that hideous war. I'm so relieved to know that you are alive, that you've come home."

Home. The word felt heavier now, and somehow entirely less hopeful than before.

THE QUEEN and Aster left me alone after that for a while, to stew in my thoughts. Part of me wondered if perhaps they were lying, but then I remembered Uncle's face when he told me I shouldn't come here.

It wasn't just about my safety, although that could easily have been in jeopardy, as well, when I was the daughter of tyrants, of warmongers. "Usurper," the princess had called me, and she only appeared to be half-joking.

Uncle had wanted to shield me from this, though, as he had so many other things. Maybe that should have made me angry, but mostly I was just really... sad. And tired, thinking about it all.

An impatient knock sounded at the door before Aster came sweeping back in. Her long, purple waves were loose and free, and somehow managed to not look at all out of place paired with her sweeping, gauzy gown. The queen followed her, as graceful as ever.

"I know you have much to think about," Cassia said. "But I wanted you to know that you can have a home here, if you wish it. You are not your parents, and we would never hold their misdeeds against you. I can't imagine what it was to be raised without a single person like you, how alone you must have felt. You don't have to go back to that," she finished, softly.

I nodded mutely, the offer bringing unexpected tears to my eyes.

My skin flashed too many colors to keep track of, and Aster chuckled softly.

"We'll need to kick that habit before we have you out and about," she said, softening it with a wink.

"I can't help it," I said, a little defensively.

"Sure, you can." She smirked, and her skin turned an amused shade of orange. My jaw dropped, and she laughed again.

"Yes," Cassia explained, her own lips turning up. "We all have the capability, but most of us learn to control it when we're children. What you're doing is rather like standing in a quiet room and shouting your emotions for the world to see."

"Or like a toddler throwing a tantrum, even," Aster added, but there was no malice in the words. "I can help you, if you'd like." The words came out a little more shyly than the rest had, and I found myself smiling in response.

"I would like that," I answered her.

"Perfect," she beamed. Then she eyed the sundress I hadn't bothered to change out of and the rat's nest that was surely my hair. "Maybe while we're at it, we can get you looking a little more like a fairy princess."

❦ 38 ❦

EDRICH

I f I thought riding Maggie was easy, flying with Pepper was something else, entirely. I held on tightly as she soared through the clouds, dipping to the left or right every so often, gliding through the air with ease.

It had been hours since we left Maggie and Rumple on the ground, more than enough time to mull over everything he'd told me and every way that might break Lina's heart. Not long ago, I'd hated the little green-and-gold man, everything he stood for and everything he was—but I couldn't hate him for this.

He had done what he had to in order to protect Lina. I couldn't fault him for that.

I risked a glance down and watched as the purple hills raced beneath us. There were mushroom circles scattered all over the ground between the flowers, growing thicker and denser the further we went. It was genius really, to even the playing field and protect themselves this way. If everyone was the same size, then the fairies weren't at a disadvantage defending their kingdom.

A part of me wondered if an ogre or centaur or dwarf had ever risked coming this way. I chuckled to myself. *Now that would be something to see.*

Pepper's wings tilted slightly, and we were soaring at a steady decline, cutting through the air like a hot blade through butter.

"I could get used to—" I started just as she leaned too far to the side and I nearly lost my balance.

"Show off," I muttered, pulling myself closer to her back.

I gripped her tighter, and while there was a part of me that was panicking about how far of a drop it was to the ground, there was another part of me that relished the feeling of flying.

Is this how Lina feels now that she has wings?

That thought was quickly replaced by another as Pepper's speed seemed to slow as we approached a large wall.

No. Not a wall. The forest?

It was hard to reconcile what I was seeing with what I knew about trees.

There were close to thirty trees with thick trunks and winding branches that seemed to be tangled together to form some sort of wall. Without my needing to guide her, Pepper flew in a circle around the outskirts, and it was the same on each side. Movement caught my eye, and I noticed a few small figures flying in through some sort of wall near the canopy. Not just figures—*but fairies.*

Small birds were flying in and out of the treetops, as well, each of them carrying some parcel in their claws and landing near what looked to be a castle carved into the massive tree in the center. Past that, there was an entire world that wound down through the trees. From this height, I could make out dozens of everyday things and places that I had taken for granted back home.

It had been hard to imagine something on this scale a few days ago, but now that just felt ignorant.

Why wouldn't a world exist that can accommodate Lina?

"This is it, Pepper. I think we've found it," I whispered, as I continued to take it all in.

We flew around the fortress one more time before I came up with what I hoped was a solid plan.

As soon as the landing platform was clear of the other birds, and the deliveries, and most of the fairies had left, I made my move. With a few gentle nudges, Pepper seemed to understand exactly what I wanted from her. It wasn't long before we were beginning our descent into what could only be Ellaria.

I plastered myself as close as I could to Pepper's back, only risking a glance every now and then to see if anyone had spotted us. Quickly, I worked my way off of her back, standing between her and one of the green spotted mushrooms to be sure I was out of sight.

A fairy with white wings and matching hair who wore small spectacles, like my father did for reading, was looking toward my falcon with confusion. He checked the list in his hand a few times before heading in our direction.

"What do we have here? I don't believe I've seen you before." His voice was calm, and that was a good sign. He wasn't suspicious. *Yet.*

The next time he glanced at his list, I made a beeline for an alcove in the grand structure on the other side of him, running as fast and as quietly as I could. Once I was certain I hadn't been spotted, I breathed a sigh of relief.

As soon as I was out of sight, Pepper spread her wings wide, and darted back up into the sky.

Good girl.

I used the moment's distraction to slip through a door behind me. Memories of the last time I visited a castle came flooding back. The family that we had delivered to the queen of Floriend; how she had ordered us to hunt them down for her. We hadn't asked why. We hadn't asked what she planned to do with them. We had taken her at her word that she wouldn't hurt them.

At the time, it felt like we didn't have a choice. Looking back, it was obvious that we did, and we made the wrong one. I would never forgive myself for that. *For any of it.*

I shook the images off and focused on the task at hand.

It wasn't long before I found my way to the living quarters. I moved down the hall, ducking in and out of the shadows, even though the floor seemed relatively empty. A door opened further down, and the sound of laughter flooded the hallway.

Though it was mingled with another voice, I wouldn't mistake that sound for anything in the world.

Sure enough, a few seconds later, Lina emerged from one of the rooms with another woman. She was dressed in a flowing, silver gown that suited her far more than the simple dresses her mother had made her. It hugged the curves I'd never known she possessed, and accented every feminine inch of her. But what stood out the most was the sparkling jewel woven into her hair.

She looked like a princess. *She is a princess.*

Their laughter echoed down the hallway, following them to wherever they were headed next.

Once I was certain they were gone, I crept into the room they'd been in. I told myself that I needed to speak with her... just to be sure that what I witnessed was real. That she really was safe. That they were treating her well. For hours, I told myself everything but the truth.

That I just want to see her—one last time.

❧ 39 ❧

LINA

As soon as we entered the ballroom, I felt as if I'd stopped breathing. Fairies flew around the room, pinning vines and streamers near the ceiling. They hung lanterns filled with glowing moss, and braided small white flowers into the vines. It looked magical.

I spun in a slow circle to take it all in. There were tables being set up around the edges of the room, and a dance floor was being polished in the middle.

"You're doing it again," Aster whispered, looking me up and down.

I groaned as I took in the pale silver color that had overtaken me, almost the exact shade of my dress. It was now shifting to a deep, shimmering pink, instead.

"Frolicking centaurs!" I cursed under my breath, and Aster laughed.

"That's one I haven't heard before. And it's okay. We'll get you used to it. Just take a deep breath in through your nose, and slowly release through your mouth three times.

Then, think about the color you want to be. Make yourself that color."

I arched my brow and stared at her.

"Don't you look at me like that." She laughed. "You're thinking about it too hard. It should come naturally."

"Fine," I said, doubtfully.

Closing my eyes, I focused on taking deep breaths in, slowly releasing again and again until she clapped her hands.

I looked down at my arms, and they were back to their neutral rose-gold.

"That's so weird." I gasped, turning them over to see if the color had spread to the other side.

"Speaking of weird. There's my brother." She pointed across the room to where the queen was standing with a few other fairies.

"Come on. Let's introduce you before we take lunch."

Without another word, she was dragging me across the floor, with the same quick pace that she seemed to do everything in.

"Lark, Lina. Lina, Lark," she said as soon as we reached the group.

Queen Cassia cleared her throat disapprovingly at her daughter, and I felt a blush rising under my skin. I quickly stifled it, using the method Aster had taught me, and was relieved to see the queen's nod of approval.

"Yes, Lina. This is my son. Prince Larkspur," she added, after a moment.

When Aster said "weird," I'd expected a gangly and awkward teenage boy, not the handsome man that stood before me.

I swallowed hard, trying to formulate a coherent

sentence while I soaked in the sight of him. He was tall and slim, but he looked strong, too. His hair was a shade darker than Aster's iris-colored tresses, and his eyes were swirling pools of amethyst and gray.

"It is a pleasure to meet you." His voice was rich and deep, and for a moment I wondered if he had been plucked directly from every fairy story I had ever read. He took my hand and bowed, placing a kiss just above my knuckles.

An awkward sound escaped my lips—one that was somewhere between a laugh and a sigh, before I remembered how to speak.

"Yes. Yes, the—erm—pleasure is mine," I said back, wanting to kick myself for how ridiculous I sounded.

Aster snorted, and Lark simply smiled, while Queen Cassia shook her head.

"Lina, you look lovely," the queen said, interrupting the awkward silence that had overtaken me.

"Thank you, Your Majesty," I said, smiling between the queen and her daughter. "Aster was so kind to share her dresses with me—"

"Are you kidding?" Aster interrupted. "I think I had more fun playing dress-up than you did."

I laughed because she wasn't wrong.

I touched the jeweled tiara self-consciously, thinking about the implications of wearing it around actual royalty.

"It suits you," Queen Cassia said, gently reaching for my hand. "Don't you think so, Son?"

My eyes widened as I fought down another blush, but Prince Larkspur didn't hesitate before responding.

"Yes, I think it suits her perfectly," he added, with a smile.

I didn't miss the way Aster and the queen shared a private grin of their own, in response, but I was grateful for another subject change when the queen spoke again.

"Why don't we adjourn for lunch?" she suggested. "Periwinkle? Crocus? I will be back afterwards to finalize the details for the ball... but for now, I think we could all use a break."

"Yes, My Queen," the fairies said in unison, with a bow.

The prince offered his arm to escort me toward the balcony. I reluctantly took it and felt a wave of varied emotions in response. He was warm and steady, and somehow being this close to him, I could feel a calm radiating off of him that helped to still my nerves.

We followed the queen out of the ballroom and onto a balcony where a table was prepared for us. I stared in wonder at the arrangement and how it was lined with plates, utensils, napkins, and decor that was all perfectly designed for us. Small cakes and bread loaves filled serving trays, and there were even chalices with wine that I could hold in one hand.

A pang went through me as I thought of the chalices back at The Poisoned Apple. They weren't made for me, but they were pretty perfect, all the same.

Lark led me to one side of the table. I took a seat, and he took the one next to me, while his mother sat across from him, and Aster across from me.

The conversation came easily, as did the laughter. Even the queen cracked a smile over Aster throwing a bit of bread at Lark's head when he made a joke at her expense.

It was comfortable and natural and enjoyable, but I still felt like I was on the outside looking in. Even though

I was beginning to be a part of a world I had always dreamt of, there was still something missing.

Someone, a traitorous voice in my head reminded me.

"So, you said that you haven't had your wings for very long?" Lark asked, after I gave them all the short version of my journey here.

"I can't say I agree with his methods, but I do understand the lengths someone would go to keep their child safe." Queen Cassia's voice was soft as she reached across the table to hold my hand. "And your wings are lovely, my dear. They seem in pristine condition in spite of the pain you must have suffered to have them stunted so."

I could feel my skin warming with embarrassment from all the attention directed at me and my new wings.

When Aster spoke up, I was grateful.

"I say we test them out. Let's go flying!"

A smile tugged at my mouth and I nodded, earning a squeal of excitement from the princess.

"Come on! There are so many things we can show you!" Aster grabbed my hand and that of her brothers, and led us to the balcony, listing off several attractions that she wanted to share.

Before I knew it, we were in the air, soaring high above Ellaria. I tried to follow Aster's lead as she spun and dove and flew like the most elegant creature I'd ever seen before.

Though flying came easily, what Aster was doing was more of a dance—one I wanted desperately to learn.

We weren't the only ones in the air. Couples held

hands, and older children flew in playful loops around each other. One couple carried a woven basket between them, and I furrowed my brow.

"It's for a baby. We don't get our wings until we're a little older." Aster's voice was in my ear, and I turned to see she had swooped close to me.

That made sense; my pain hadn't started until I was closer to my teenage years.

Sure enough, when we passed over the couple, I caught sight of a tiny sleeping fairy, a serene shade of pale pink.

I couldn't help but laugh. There was so much in this world to see and know and discover. I felt a small pang of sadness, though, too—one I didn't want to delve too deeply into.

Fortunately, another distraction was right around the bend, *literally*. When we flew over to the other side of the great tree, there was a group of fairies around our ages playing a game of some sort.

They were mid-air and using branches as a sort of goal posts? It reminded me of the children playing stick ball back in the village. I had always wanted to join in, but for obvious reasons, it hadn't been possible.

A pang went through me as I thought of Edrich and how he would sit each game out when I was around, even though I knew he was one of the best players. *No wonder he grew to resent me.*

Lark's voice pulled me from the memory.

"Do you want to play?"

I couldn't hide the grin that stretched across my face while I nodded.

Moments later, we were in the thick of it, Aster and Lark doing their best to explain the rules.

"You throw the mossball to your partner, and they have to hit it with the stalk out of the enemies territory. As soon as the mossball is airbound, you have to fly to that tree there." Aster pointed to the tree on the other side of the clearing. "Got it?"

"I think so." I answered, replaying what she said and what I had seen of the game already.

Before I knew it, it was my turn with the stalk, and Lark was throwing the mossball in my direction.

I had never played any sport before. There had never been one I could join in, so I really wasn't expecting to hit the ball on the first try. Somehow, though, the stalk connected solidly with the little green ball.

Lark and Aster were yelling for me to fly to our home tree, while the other team chased after the mossball. Dropping the stalk, I flew as fast as I could to the tree and back.

Our team cheered when I made it to them before the other team could score a point. Aster and Lark tackled me, throwing their arms around my shoulders while laughing.

Warmth spread throughout my limbs at their touch. *How many times have I seen my friends do something similar?* It was so small, and so simple, but even though we were flying, their arms around me grounded me in a way I never knew was possible.

Gradually, I saw the other members of our team loosen up where I was concerned, also. There was a tightness in their shoulders that eased with each interaction, and I wondered if there was more than one reason Lark and Aster had wanted to join in this game.

When the game was over, we flew to the top of the canopy to watch the sunset on the valley.

"I'm going to miss this." Lark sighed.

"What do you mean? Is something happening to Ellaria?" A moment of panic seized me.

"No, no. Nothing like that–" Lark began before Aster cut him off.

"He's just upset about being forced to marry. He has to choose his bride by the night of the ball." She said and Lark gently pushed her.

"Not upset. It is my responsibility, one I'm happy to take on... but, things will change and I can only hope it will be for the better." He added before pointing toward the horizon.

I thought over his words and found that bittersweet sentiment seeping deep in my bones, before an array of colors spread out before us.

Beams of apricot and rose-colored light highlighted the purple hills surrounding the border of Ellaria in a spectacular array of color. It was the most lovely sunset I had ever seen.

And in spite of the day, being so accepted into this family, spending time with people like me in a world suited for us... there was a traitorous part of my heart that felt selfish for wanting more.

I scanned the valley below from the Enchanted Forest, past the violet covered hills, and my chest tightened. I hadn't realized I was holding my breath, until Aster nudged me.

"You all right, Lina?" she asked, and I nodded.

It was a lie.

Here I was, surrounded by everything I had ever wanted or dreamt of, and all I could think about was how much I wished Edrich was here to see it, too.

❧ 40 ☙

EDRICH

I stood against the wall behind Lina's door, so that no one could see me if she opened it. It was the perfect vantage point to study her luxurious room. The intricately carved furniture had been designed with her size in mind.

Piles of fabric were strewn carelessly across the short, plush couch, like she had tried on one outfit after another. There was an ornate vanity cluttered with cosmetics and jewels sparkling in the moonlight coming through her window.

It was a happy sort of mess, and the longer she was gone, the more time I had to convince myself there was no point in me being here. I had seen her, not only safe, but *laughing*, with others like her, just like she had always wanted.

So why haven't I left yet?

I told myself it was because she may have been putting on a show, that I couldn't go until she told me herself that she was okay. *But even I don't believe it.*

When her door finally opened, I felt an unexpected

bundle of nerves in the pit of my stomach. She had left me in that valley, and she probably didn't want to see me now. I had just enough time to regret my decision to stay before she walked in and pulled the door shut behind her.

Her back was to me, and I knew I should call out and let her know I was here, but she looked so sad, like she had deflated the moment she was alone. Her magnificent wings were drooping behind her, her bare hands a pale blue-gray, as they pulled her tiara from her head and tossed it on the sofa with more force than I would have expected.

Did something happen?

When her fingers moved to the buttons on the back of her dress, I finally made myself move, creating just enough noise to alert her.

"Lina," I said softly, trying not to startle her.

She whipped around, her skin already shining such a brilliant silver, it was hard to look at her.

"Edrich?" Her lips parted in surprise. Emotions flitted through her eyes, confusion and surprise and something that might have been relief. Not anger, though. "How?"

It took me a moment to answer her, because even in the wan light of the moon, she was... perfect. With huge eyes and a pert, upturned nose, she was every bit as gorgeous as she had ever been—but so much more real now that she was right in front of me, the same size. *Well, almost,* I mentally amended. She was still about half a head shorter than I was.

"Mushroom gas," I finally croaked out.

She nodded slowly.

"Pixie dust," she mumbled, more to herself than me, the shock still evident in her eyes.

She strode almost subconsciously toward me, her hand

outstretched. I didn't move—I couldn't, not when she was running her fingers gently along my hairline, then the side of my face, like she was still trying to convince herself this wasn't a hallucination.

I knew the feeling, but I didn't trust myself to reach out and touch her. As it was, I could barely breathe. I knew, then. *This is why I haven't been able to make myself leave.*

Because I had spent the better part of a decade wondering what it might be like if Lina and I were the same size, and maybe it was selfish of me, but I had to see her this way—at least once.

She pulled her hand back once she realized what she was doing, pressing her fingertips gently to her mouth instead.

"I can't believe you're here. And little, like me." She seemed to be trying to collect herself, her skin flashing too many colors for me to keep up with, until she settled into something neutral. "Why *are* you here?"

She may as well have doused me with a bucket of cold water, the matter-of-fact way she asked. I blinked a couple of times, not sure why I was surprised. She had made her feelings clear enough when she floated away without a word in the valley.

Clearing my throat, I gave her the same half-baked answer I had given myself.

"I had to make sure you were safe, before I left."

"Oh." She stood up a little straighter, her chin lifting as she gestured around her. "Well, as you can see, I'm great."

"I *can* see that." My voice was as hollow as the rest of me felt. Some small part of me had acknowledged the inevitability of this moment from the day she asked me to come with her to find the fairies, but it didn't make it any less excruciating now that it was here.

I tried to shake this feeling off. She was happy, and I was happy for her. After all, she had finally found her people.

Now, I just need to find a way to get back to mine.

❊ 41 ❊

LINA

I tried not to stare at Edrich, tried to remind myself to breathe. *Is it possible that he looks even more handsome this size?*

It felt like we were living out one of the fantasies I had stopped even dreaming about, years ago.

Or at least, it had felt that way before he opened his mouth.

Now I studied him, searching for a single sign of warmth, of the friend I thought I had all those years, and coming up short. His features were guarded, even when he let loose a sigh.

"Truly, Lina, I'm glad you found what you were looking for."

Have I? I wasn't sure, but I wasn't about to admit that to him. He had stolen enough of my pride with his lies and manufactured feelings. He was probably only here because Uncle forced him to come as some last remnant of the deal.

What had he said? *I had to.* I supposed that was the

story of our lives, where he was concerned. Uncharacter-istic bitterness swept through me, but I fought to keep my tone neutral when I responded.

"I guess we both did," I finally said.

I had found the fairies, and he had found a way to save his father—a way that didn't involve being stuck to me.

His face grew even more tense. There was a prolonged silence, one that felt weighted down with everything I couldn't bring myself to say or ask, before he gave a terse nod.

"Rumplestiltskin got big again, so there must be a way. Can we ask one of the royals, then I can head back?" He turned toward the door.

Panic surged up in my chest. I didn't want him to leave right now, on these terms. *What if I never see him again?* I grasped around for something, anything, to keep him from leaving like this.

"They've all gone to bed," I fibbed. "Besides, it would be dangerous, traveling this late. Just... stay here, and we'll ask them in the morning." *Does he hear the pleading in my voice as plainly as I do?*

"You want me to stay in your bedroom?" His tone was perfectly neutral.

"We shared a tent. This is the same thing. Besides, we used to have sleepovers all the time when we were little." I reminded him, daring him to say how this was any differ-ent, to put voice to any one of the hundreds of thoughts flitting around my head.

He opened his mouth to respond, then closed it. Several blinks later, he nodded, though there was a kind of challenge in his eyes.

"Of course. This is just like that." Was I imagining that mocking lilt to his words?

We both turned to look at the bed, and still, neither of us moved. My limbs were actually frozen in the awkwardness of how to approach getting into bed, whether I should change into my nightclothes. Would it be weirder if I didn't, or if I did?

"I'll just take the floor," Edrich muttered.

"Of course," I said, like that was obvious to me. And it should have been, would have been, if I hadn't been so flustered by the whole situation. *Right?*

Edrich turned around while I changed, the only sounds in the room the slide of silky fabric against skin and his carefully measured breaths. By the time I crawled into bed, I was grateful for the way I could hide beneath the blanket.

I tossed him one of my pillows, and he laid on the floor as far from my bed as he could get. I couldn't help but steal glances at him while he stared up at the ceiling.

He looked somehow more real than usual, starlight from the window illuminating the lines of exhaustion in his face. Or maybe it was just because he was my size now, and I could see him a little more clearly.

When it became evident that neither of us was sleeping, I shattered the fitful silence.

"How did you even get here?" I asked.

He didn't startle at the sound of my voice, didn't turn his head, just grunted out a single word. "Pepper."

I guess he didn't feel like talking. But that left me alone with my thoughts going to traitorous places, like wondering at the risk of riding a bird when you didn't have wings to catch you if you fell. Wondering if someone would do something like that on obligation alone, then catching sight of Edrich's hardened features and cursing myself for falling down the same familiar rabbit holes.

"Is Uncle all right?"

He sighed, like even talking to me was a burden. I echoed his sigh with one of my own, but he eventually responded.

"Yes. He was riding Maggie. They should be here soon." There was a note of finality in his tone, and I finally decided to take the hint that he didn't want to talk.

Even if I did wonder why, when Uncle was on his way, Edrich came, as well. Risked his life to come faster, for that matter.

I thought about what I had asked him. *Did you ever think about what it would be like if we were the same size?*

It was all I thought about.

But here we were, and I had never felt farther away from him.

❧ 42 ❧

EDRICH

I was awakened to the sound of a chipper voice that was decidedly not Lina.

"Let's go shopping this morning!" The door thumped shut, and I wondered how I had slept through it being opened. In fairness, though, it had been a long night of churning thoughts and second-guesses before I finally passed out.

"Um... " Lina's groggy response was cut off by a scandalized gasp.

"Where is your other pillow?" the voice whisper-yelled, though I wasn't sure why she bothered when I had tested the soundproofness of the room myself yesterday.

"I—" Whatever lie Lina was concocting, badly, she didn't get the chance to finish, before a girl flitted around the side of the bed, looking down at me with interest.

Purple waves tumbled down around a pretty, heart-shaped face with delicate features. What I could see of her wings was a glimmering periwinkle, and they were rounder than Lina's. Her most obvious feature, though, was the mischievous smirk she was shooting my way.

"It's not what you think, Aster," Lina said.

I stood up, trying to get my clothes back in order.

"Clearly." Aster shook her head in mock dismay. "Since you're both still fully clothed. Which is a waste, I tell you. An absolute waste." She raked her eyes up and down my body.

"I—" I started to say something, though I wasn't quite sure what, when Aster interrupted me.

"You might want to put that pillow back, though," she chirped. "Mother's nearly here."

Sure enough, only moments later there was a lighter knock at the door. Lina shook her head, and I flung the pillow back on her bed just as the door was opening.

I hastily smoothed out my hair just in time to meet the Queen of Ellaria. An elegant woman entered, all shades of cinnamon and cream, and exuding the kind of warmth my own mother always did.

"Mama," the girl, who I realized now was *Princess* Aster, said cheerily. "Lina has been fortunate enough to find one of her companions, and it looks like the mushrooms are still working admirably to protect our little kingdom."

The queen eyed me as I bowed, not distrustfully, exactly, but she did take in my rumpled clothes and bare feet.

"I see. I must apologize for the sentries," she said, sincerely. "Old prejudices die hard, I'm afraid, though we are no longer in the habit of leaving those who are subjected to the gas out in the valley to be eaten."

"That's... good to hear," I floundered, still off-footed from this whole exchange.

Not that I had never encountered a queen before. *Just never one with a single shred of decency.*

"So you have a way to make me big again?" Why did my chest feel tight when I asked that?

She nodded. "You are welcome to the tonic which restores your molecules to their original state, so long as you swear an oath on your life to never reveal the existence or location of Ellaria."

"Of course," I rasped out. The queen gave me a waiting expression, and I said the rest. "I swear on my life to never reveal the existence or location of Ellaria."

She held my gaze with her own assessing one, before nodding.

"I'll have the tonic brought as soon as you are ready to leave. It works instantly, so be sure you're clear of Ellaria before you drink it. No need to terrify our citizens with a giant in their midst." Her eyes twinkled with amusement.

Clear of Ellaria. Of course I had planned to leave, but this felt like it was happening so fast. I couldn't quite bring myself to respond, and Lina was similarly close-mouthed.

Aster looked shrewdly between us before she broke the awkward silence.

"Mama, he can't get big again until after the ball. It will give Lina a chance to say farewell to her friend, and me a chance to have a date other than the stuffy courtiers I go with every year." She smirked.

The queen eyed her a bit indulgently.

"Aster, Darling, have you even asked our guest if he even wants to stay that long?"

"Please," Aster looked at me. "It's just tomorrow night."

I looked at Lina, still sleepy-faced and wide-eyed, skin

a pale shade of silver I couldn't quite interpret. I could have given myself a thousand excuses, from manners to ensuring Lina really was safe, but I didn't bother. I knew I wasn't quite ready to leave yet, even if I was making things worse for myself in the end.

"I'd be happy to." I dipped my head at Aster.

"Perfect!"

"Oh, and Lina, Dear?" The queen arched an eyebrow.

"Yes?" Lina spoke at last, her voice pitched unnaturally high.

"Next time a *guest* of yours arrives in the middle of the night, you know we would be happy to show him to one of the suites. Aster, you can do that now, in fact." She turned back to Lina. "Any friend of yours is welcome any time, but perhaps the room of an unmarried princess is not the ideal place for him to stay."

With that, the queen swept out of the room.

Aster exchanged a look with Lina that clearly said, *Yikes.*

"Don't worry," she said. "She knows nothing happened or even she would have lost control of her colors. She already thinks of you as family, you know, and sometimes, that will mean getting chastised in front of your sexy little human friend with a handful of guards outside when you forget *decorum.*"

"Thanks, Aster." Lina blanched, but didn't say anything else in response.

"Anywho, you can dress for breakfast, Lina. I need to take this one to get fitted for a tux for the ball." The princess looked me up and down before adding. "And something to wear for our outing today."

Without another word, she grabbed ahold of my arm and tugged me toward the door.

ASTER HAD BEEN GIVING me a look far too scrutinizing for my liking while the tailor, Buckthorne, poked and prodded me, pulling his measuring tape around every part of my body.

"I would never really go on a date with someone who spent the night with my friend, you know," she blurted out casually, when the man stepped out of the room.

In spite of my generally black mood, I found myself smiling at her unveiled honesty, wanting to return it.

"Well, I would never really go on a date with the friend of someone I spent the night with," I said darkly. Whether it had been technically platonic, Aster clearly knew there were complications. "But it does make me question why you wanted me to stay."

I fixed her with a stare as bold as the one she was giving me. She reminded me of my brother—direct, perceptive, and guileless. Sure enough, she gave me an answer.

"Because I like Lina, and I suspect that she would be sad if you left so soon."

I bit back a sigh. Lina was the last thing I wanted to talk about right now. *Or think about.*

Buckthorne walked back in with a three-piece tuxedo, saving us both from an awkward silence. He held it up against me, muttering to himself.

"So." Aster raised her aubergine-colored eyebrows, letting me know she knew I wanted her to change the subject, but had no intention of doing so. "How long have you known Lina?"

"As long as I can remember," I answered.

Maybe that is why it's so hard to imagine a life without her.

"It shouldn't be too much trouble to fix something up for him," the thin, balding man with short, round wings finally said, interrupting my thoughts. "Though we'll have to sew up the wing slits." His tone told me that was an insult, and I remembered the queen's words about old prejudices dying hard.

Aster only rolled her eyes.

"Obviously," she said, still eyeing me like she was trying to solve a particularly interesting puzzle.

We left then, and she tugged me along to a corridor not far from the one Lina was staying in, stopping outside one of the doors.

"This is your room." Aster swung the door open to reveal a stately room, decorated in tiny navy and yellow flowers. "Everything you need should be in here, but just let someone know if there's anything else you want. Or *anyone*." She smirked.

"Thank you, but I'm sure I'm just fine," I said, a little too forcefully.

She only shrugged, leaving me at last to be alone with my thoughts.

✺ 43 ✺

LINA

ster came to fetch me for breakfast, merrily informing me that Edrich was cleaning up and changing and that she had sent food to his room. I had seen the gleam of speculation in her eyes when she asked him to stay for the ball, and I didn't think she was being conniving for her own sake, as much as mine.

Still, I couldn't help but ask. "So, you and Edrich... at the ball?" *Real subtle, Lina.*

Aster's gentle laughter chimed through the air, and she linked her arm in mine. "Well I haven't known you long, but I thought you might murder me if I asked him to stay to be *your* date." She paused, assessing my features with a sweeping glance. "And I got the feeling you weren't quite ready to say goodbye to him."

A tightness in my chest eased at her words. I told myself it wasn't the easing of jealousy, so much as that she was right, I hadn't been ready to say goodbye. *Now I have another day to do that.*

"We've been friends for a long time," was all I said. "Nothing more."

"Mhmm." She didn't so much agree, as let me drop the subject. "Well, on that note, I want you to know that I'm glad you're here. That whatever you decide, or whoever you're... more than friends with, I hope you'll stay. Everyone else here is boring." She winked an amethyst eye, dropping my arm to open the dining hall door.

I would have pushed her on it, but we were the last ones to breakfast. Cassia and Lark were already seated, looking expectantly at us.

I could always ask her about it later.

IT SURPRISED me all over again how there was no awkwardness around the royal family—as if I had known them my entire life. The queen laughed and asked questions, while Aster and Lark filled her in on yesterday, and I chimed in to give my side of things.

Until Aster was in the middle of talking about the ball, and Cassia abruptly decided that she and her daughter were needed elsewhere.

"There are a few more details that need to be seen to before the ball tomorrow. Would you mind helping me?"

"What details?" Aster asked, around a large bite of a sweet cream tart.

"I can explain on the way," the queen said, with a small arch of her brow.

"If there is anything I can do to help—" I started.

"No, my dear. You are our guest. Larkspur will keep you company until we return."

Aster glanced back and forth between us, a slightly resigned grin spreading over her mouth.

"All right, Larky. Don't you go stealing her away from me, now. She was my friend first, even if Lina perhaps finds you to be a little easier on the eyes," she said, waggling her eyebrows at us before joining her mother.

I could hear Cassia scolding her about etiquette and being discreet once the doors were closed. A blush heated my skin before I could help it, but Lark was kind enough to pretend not to notice.

"That's my sister for you."

"I love her for it." I laughed softly.

"I can tell you mean that." He gave me a genuine smile. "I hope you'll stay here with us."

It was a curious echo of what Aster had said, and I began to have a sneaking suspicion of what she had been alluding to.

"I plan to," I told him, honestly.

"Good. You belong here, and the people already love you."

Suddenly the open-aired balcony felt claustrophobic as everything I had been pondering clicked firmly into place.

"Have you chosen anyone for the ball?" It was as close as I could come to asking what I wanted to know.

"No one definitive." He cast a speculative glance my way, one that reminded me so much of Aster I almost let out an impractical giggle.

"And you," he asked. "Are you taking your... friend?"

"No!" I practically shouted. "I mean, Aster is taking him. Edrich and me... we grew up together."

"So there's nothing more... between you?" He floundered a bit awkwardly, and it was endearing enough that I smiled before sadness chased the expression away.

I thought about all the things Edrich and I had said in the forest, then I thought about the reality of our situation, before settling on what felt like the truth.

"No. He's leaving after the ball, in fact. He only came to make sure I was safe."

There was a silence while Lark surveyed the breathtaking view, water droplets falling from one shiny green leaf to another so quickly it was like a waterfall just our size.

"Do you believe in fate, Lina?"

My stomach twisted.

"No, I can't say that I do. I believe we make our own choices, right or wrong, and live with the results." I grimaced because it sounded exactly like something Edrich would say.

Lark nodded and leaned toward me. There was a sincerity in his eyes that hadn't been there before.

"You don't think it could be fate that you wound up in Ellaria just before I was supposed to choose a bride? You, the daughter of Queen Hyacinth, who many people still feel loyalty to?"

My chest tightened.

"I can't say that is fate, so much as a very, very unlikely, improbable, unrealistic coincidence," I said, and he laughed.

"That could be." He brought a finger up to his temple. "But consider it for just a moment, from my perspective. I'm not claiming to have fallen in love with you in the day since we met. I'm simply wondering how such an opportunity presented itself just before I make an important decision. There is still some unrest within the kingdom. I wonder if those who miss your parents' rule would be satisfied with our alliance."

I was impressed that I was able to keep my skin neutral throughout this entire conversation, because I felt anything but calm inside.

"Is this something that you actually want? You don't even know me." My voice was steady, though my heart was breaking.

I wished I could pretend I didn't know why, that I wasn't fully aware of what kept me from being excited by the prospect of a life here with the charming prince and his perfect family. *A family that would be mine in truth, if I said yes.*

"I want what is best for Ellaria. And Mother... well, between the rebellions and the way she is half ready to adopt you, I believe she might have hopes in that direction, though she hasn't directly mentioned it."

I must have blanched a bit, because he held out a hand.

"Please, don't misunderstand me. My mother is very fond of you, regardless of anything that happens between us."

I couldn't deny the relief seeping over me. At least, there had been no subterfuge. Just a typical mother, wanting to see her son married off. I could hardly blame her for that.

"And you?" I forced myself to ask. "This isn't a decision that should be made for other people. It should be something that you want."

He considered me seriously for a moment.

"There's nothing set in stone, despite my parents' urging for the past few years. And though we don't know each other well, I already feel like we're friends. Like we could be even better friends, with time... and maybe even more than that." He sighed. "Isn't that what anyone wants in a partner?"

His words sent an unexpected pang through me.

Friends. Best friends. *That would make for an ideal relationship.*

"Yes." I let out a slow breath. "I think you and I could be very good friends."

"So maybe we owe it to ourselves to consider it, then," he added, after a moment.

I thought about what he was offering me. A future with a kind, considerate husband. A family. And one day, *a kingdom.*

Then I thought about my reasons for hesitating, and how they hinged on a man who had been forced to look after me and was going back to being roughly a hundred times my size in a day.

I would be an idiot not to at least think it over.

"That much, I can promise you."

🌱 44 🌿

EDRICH

I munched on a tiny scone, marveling at how much richer everything tasted at this size, like it was in a super concentrated form. I thought about how comfortable my loose tunic and leggings were, how even though I was indoors, it felt fresh and open with all the flowers, less claustrophobic feeling than the average room.

Mostly, I thought about anything and everything I could to avoid thinking about Lina, or why I had agreed to stay here when I knew it would make walking away that much harder.

I was grateful when a rapid knock at the door interrupted my thoughts. Aster barged in before I answered, the same way she had to Lina's room.

"What if I had been changing?" I demanded.

"Then we would have both been scandalized. Alas, we would have found some way to move forward." She placed a dramatic arm on her forehead and I couldn't help but laugh.

"Are you ready?" she asked.

"For what?"

"To come shopping with me and Lina."

"Um, I didn't realize... "

"Well you don't want to be stuck in this stuffy room all day, do you?"

This room wasn't stuffy, but she had a point. *It's not like I have anything else to do.*

"Of course not." I kept my tone wry to show her I knew she was plotting. "I guess I'm ready, then."

She smirked, like she knew exactly what I hadn't said.

"Perfect. Lina!" Aster yelled, and I saw a sentry behind her shake his head in amusement. "Let's go!"

I OFFERED to call Pepper from the balcony and fly her around, but Aster shook her head.

"We can just take the lift," she said.

She was the only one talking. Lina and I hadn't exchanged more than a few uncomfortable glances, but Aster seemed content to carry the conversation and pretend to be oblivious to that fact.

The lift, as it turned out, was a series of platforms and pulley systems tied to ropes in a complicated rig that eventually led to the ground.

At least, I assume it does.

We weren't alone. A few elderly fairies with slightly drooping wings joined us, as well as a family with small children.

Aster made conversation with all of them as we made our slow descent, leaving Lina and I to stare anywhere but at each other.

"Is your brother coming?" Lina asked Aster, when there was a lull in the chatter.

Her brother, the prince? Does Lina sound hopeful that he will be here?

"No, he has boring heir things to do today, but I'm free. Perks of being the spare." Aster shrugged and smiled, and Lina shook her head.

When we reached the ground, I took a moment to assess the creatures pulling the ropes. Guinea pigs, I thought, though I had never seen one quite so... close. *Or big.*

I had a moment of reservation about the woodland animals being harnessed in the makeshift wheels connected to the rig, but they didn't seem to be any different than the beasts of burden on a farm, or any less happy.

Several fairies watched the animals at work, fanning them with giant leaves, or funneling water into a bowl for them to drink from.

"Satisfied?" Lina asked. It was the first real thing she had said to me since leaving, but there was no ire in it. If anything, her lips curved up in a truce of sorts.

"More or less," I said, giving her a half smile of my own.

Aster looked between us quizzically, and Lina explained.

"Edrich loves animals," she said. "He always checks to make sure they're being treated properly. He was always fixing up the animals on the farm for me."

"Oh, we're very serious about taking care of our little helpers," Aster said. Then, with an apologetic look at Lina, she added, "At least, the Thandrians are."

Lina gave a resigned sort of grimace, enough to tell me that she was already aware of what Rumplestiltskin had told me about her family. And that once again, we had both underestimated her, because she was not broken.

Not even close.

Aster pulled me from my thoughts with an excited squeal. "Oh, look, we can go talk to their healer and you can see for yourself!"

She tugged us over to a man who was crouched at the foot of one of the guinea pigs, whispering soothing things under his breath as the creature squealed.

Aster stopped short, clearly not wanting to interrupt him, but I moved closer to see what he was doing. A huge splinter was embedded in the guinea pig's paw, and the fairy was struggling to pull it out and sooth the creature at the same time.

I stepped forward without hesitation. This couldn't be much different than dealing with farm animals. I crouched in front of the man, reaching toward the animal.

"May I?"

His bright orange gaze swept over my clearly wingless back, then to my companions before he gave a wary nod.

Reaching forward, I firmly grasped the guinea pig's ankle, murmuring a few gentle assurances. The fairy used his now free hand to wrench the splinter out in one solid tug. He dabbed some ointment on the wound, and bandaged it, all while I kept the animal still and calm.

"Thank you," he said. "You've a knack for that."

"There weren't many formal animal healers in the village," I shrugged.

The man nodded in understanding. "It's hard to find

good help here, what with a few old prejudices about our helpers here. How long are you here?"

It wasn't hard to surmise I was an outsider, what with my being human and all, I guess.

"Just until tomorrow," I said, feeling Lina's eyes on me as I spoke.

"That's too bad," the fairy said. "If you change your mind and are looking for something to pass the time, I'm sure Aster can tell you where to find me."

His offer stopped me in my tracks. I was saved from any kind of a response when Aster flitted over to speak to him, pulling Lina along with her.

Which was just as well, of course, because the idea was ludicrous. I had a family. *Who are taken care of between Lina's farm and the money you left them,* an annoying voice in my head tacked on. And I was a sworn member of the Huntsmen. *Which you hate,* the voice added.

Finally, I forced myself to look over at Lina. For all that I was in turmoil, her skin was a perfectly neutral rose-gold.

My heart sank, some hope I hadn't realized I had dissipating in her complete lack of reaction.

Like I said, the idea was ludicrous.

❧ 45 ❧

LINA

It was hard to control my coloring as I watched Edrich tend to the poor guinea pig. Seeing his features so clearly, so close, the nuances in his expression—the thoughtful way his brow furrowed and the tilt of his mouth—it stirred something painful inside me.

I tried to shake the feeling away, but it didn't help when I would catch his eye and see the same expression mirrored there.

Did I imagine his moment of hesitation when the healer mentioned needing help?

My breathing was uneven as my mind raced in circles running through too many possibilities that would probably never come about.

Fortunately, Aster was astounding at providing distractions.

Soon after leaving the healer, she had us dashing from one shop to the next in a mad sprint.

First was the dressmakers, where she purchased tunics

and trousers and dresses, for every occasion, that she deemed would look perfect with my hair or complexion.

Telling her it was all too much was a waste of breath. She just ignored me, already on her way to the next stop.

Wherever we went, though, we had a sea of eyes watching us. Gasps came from the shoppers and vendors as they commented on my wings. I didn't miss the way Edrich stood protectively close by, or the way his eyes assessed everyone who recognized me to determine if they were a threat.

Ever the soldier, even now.

The more I looked around at the fairies surrounding us, the more I understood why Uncle said that people would recognize me for my wings. There were wings in every size and shape and color, it seemed, but none of them were iridescent like mine.

Mixed into the comments about me or my wings, were ones about the *human* in our midst. Several uttered the word disdainfully, while others sounded only curious.

The longer we shopped and the more Aster treated us normally, the less of an attraction we became for the others. Eventually they began to drift further away, allowing us some modicum of privacy.

It felt a little easier to breathe then. I was used to being a spectacle for being so small, but usually those observing me were much bigger, and felt further away. Here, it was different. More personal and claustrophobic, somehow.

Aster's shopping cycle continued with hats and shoes and jewelry, even weaponry, much to Edrich's delight, until we eventually begged her for a rest.

"Fine, you two hang out here and I'll be back after I finish up, then," she said, before flitting away once more.

The tension between Edrich and myself had lessened throughout the day with each passing glance or comment, but now that Aster was gone, there was an awkward void between us that was hard to know how to fill.

I opened and closed my mouth a few times, trying to decide what to say when Edrich pointed to a large red and white spotted mushroom. Fairies dipped their heads out of the small windows carved into the stalk, passing out small plates of food to paying customers.

"Hungry?" he asked.

"Do you even have to ask?"

His answering smile made my heart thunder in my chest.

Frolicking Centaurs... get it together, Lina.

When we had a sampling of several specialties, and a large canister of fairy Sangria, we walked over to a small stream that wound around the great tree.

We chose a spot by the water, tasting a bit of everything, making conversation in bits and spurts as if we were amenable strangers.

While the food was spectacular, the Sangria stole the show. We made it a game to see who could eat the most fruit from the wine the fastest and found ourselves laughing like children as we fought over the final piece.

I managed to grab the last bit of strawberry when Edrich wrenched it from my grasp and popped it into his mouth with wild abandon.

"Hey!" I laughed, and pushed his arm. "That's cheating!"

"And I'm not even a little bit sorry." He threw his head back in laughter.

I hadn't seen him this carefree in years. Was it the missing weight of his obligation to me that made it so much easier for him to breathe, or was there another reason he seemed almost... at home here?

As beautiful as Ellaria was, it was hard to focus on it when all I could watch was Edrich taking it all in.

His eyes roved over the great tree, his neck bending and straining to look all the way up to the canopy. He watched families picnicking near the stream in front of us and the laughing children playing with a tree frog near the water.

Being my size gave me new things to notice about him. The subtleties in his expression, or the small quirk of his lips when he was amused.

I could watch him this way forever. *And yet, he's leaving me tomorrow...*

Edrich turned from watching a bumblebee dusting itself in pollen to find me staring. I thought he would call me out on it like he always did, but instead, his expression was thoughtful.

When his eyes caught mine, I couldn't look away. I didn't want to.

In the silent seconds that passed, there was more honesty between us than had ever been there before, and I didn't want it to ever end.

❧ 46 ❧

EDRICH

I
t was hard to believe I was leaving this place, leaving Lina for good, in just a day. Not that I had any reason to believe she wanted me to stay, even if tonight had been the most fun I had allowed myself in years.

The moon was high in the sky and I was just changing into my borrowed nightclothes when I heard a tentative knock on the door. I finished pulling the tunic over my head, but didn't bother lacing it before I pulled open the door.

Lina was standing there, a bottle of wine and two glasses in her hand. Her teal eyes roved down to my open laces and back up to my eyes, her lips parting.

"I thought—," her voice came out raspy. She swallowed, trying again. "Since tomorrow is the ball, it's your last real night here. I thought we could enjoy a pilfered bottle of wine, for old time's sake."

Her lips tugged up at the sides, but there was apprehension in her eyes. I stepped back, inviting her in.

"You didn't steal that bottle." I chuckled.

"Well, no," she admitted. "But that sounded better."

We sank down into the two armchairs by the window and I opened the bottle, pouring us each a glass.

"We used to just drink directly from the bottle," I reminded her.

"Ah, yes, but look how civilized we've become." She smirked, but something in it was forced. *Maybe like me, she feels the weight of what little time we have left hanging over us.*

The memories washed through me, then. Maybe it was because I was leaving soon, or maybe because we had felt like friends today for the first time in so long. Hell, maybe it was the Sangria, but suddenly I couldn't stop the onslaught of images of a lifetime spent with Lina.

The two of us sitting on the sidelines of a stickball game, loudly commentating on the plays and calling out the score. Patching up wounded animals together, her using her tiny hands to extract splinters or soothing the animal, while I administered stitches. Sitting down for dinner with either of our families, and the way everything had always felt so easy, so right, except for the way it never could be.

"I miss her," Lina said abruptly, pulling me from my thoughts. Her color had gone pale blue.

"I miss her, too, for what it's worth. I'm so sorry that you had to go through that. That I wasn't... there."

Lina met my eyes, and I could already see the question burning in hers, even before it came out of her mouth.

"Why weren't you there?"

That wasn't a story I wanted to tell, especially not tonight. I was silent, deliberating, when she spoke again in a quiet voice.

"I've been racking my brain, trying to put the pieces

together. I believe that there was a time our friendship was real. I want to believe that even with all the complications of your deal with Uncle, there were times it was true later."

"It was, Lina." I tried to will the truth into my voice, wanting her to hear it for what it was.

"Then where were you?"

I took a deep breath. Maybe I didn't feel like telling this story, but she deserved the truth this time. "I was in a dungeon, chained to a wall because of an evil woman who doesn't like to hear the word *no*."

Her eyes widened in horror, and I held a hand up.

"No, I don't want sympathy. I just want you to understand that I couldn't possibly have known what to say to you after that, how to explain that when your world had just fallen apart. So, writing you those five words... it was all I could do," I admitted. "Do you see now why I don't like to talk about my job?"

There was no sound aside from her carefully labored breaths while she processed everything I had just thrown at her.

"I do see," she finally said. "What I don't understand is why you would take a job like that. Were you so desperate to get away from... home?" She had been about to ask if I was so desperate to get away from her, I was sure.

I clenched my jaw, trying to find a way to make her understand, to take away some of her hurt without giving up every last damaged piece of myself.

"It wasn't always like that," I muttered. "The job, I mean." In a louder tone, I asked her, "Did you ever think that maybe I left for your sake? *Because* I cared?" I was dancing perilously close to things I didn't plan on revealing, but I couldn't seem to stop myself.

"*For my sake?*" she muttered, in disbelief, before flashing an alarming shade of crimson.

"No, Edrich." She stood up, like she couldn't contain her aggravation sitting down. "If you had left for me, you would have explained it. You would have talked to me. You would have written. You left for *your* sake."

"And how would that explanation have gone, Lina?" I got to my feet also, frustrated at her, and at myself, and at the way we kept dancing around the truth.

Mostly with myself, though, because I had managed to convince us both that I resented her when the only thing I had ever really resented was not being able to find a way for us to be together.

"You tell me," she shot back.

We were standing closer now, and I found myself having to look anywhere but her face, just so I could focus enough to answer. Whatever else was true about our situation, I knew that I owed her that much.

"All right."

"What?" She tilted her head like she thought she had heard me wrong, but I nodded.

"All right, I'll tell you how that would have gone."

It felt like time stopped in that tenuous moment, that endless space of possibility, but I was too far in to stop myself now.

"If I had given you the truth, then, it would have been this. I wanted a future with you. Wanted it more than I had ever wanted anything else, and I didn't care about our sizes, didn't care that we could never have... " Talking about a physical relationship when she was standing in front of me in a gauzy dress that hugged her perfect body like a glove felt like juggling with double edged knives, so I hedged. "A traditional relationship. You were my best friend, and I thought that would be enough."

"And then you, what?" she asked, in a voice so quiet I could hardly make out the words. "Changed your mind?"

"Not exactly." I still couldn't look at her. "My mother told me that it would be a disservice to you, to shackle you to me when there might be someone out there who could give you a real life, a full life, children and... " I trailed off, fighting the color in my cheeks.

There was a stilted silence before she responded.

"Didn't you think I deserved a say?"

I finally forced myself to meet her eyes, and I was utterly unprepared for what I saw in them. True, there was still anger swirling in their teal depths, but there was so much more—things I couldn't identify any more than I could the myriad of colors washing over her skin.

"And what would you have said?" I asked, in a voice I hardly recognized.

The inches between us seemed to crackle with electricity, our ragged breaths the only sound in the otherwise silent room. Her gaze searched mine, and I might have stopped breathing entirely while I waited for the answer to the question I had thought about every day for three years.

47

LINA

For all that Aster had been coaching me in regulating my colors, I couldn't seem to find an ounce of that control now.

He had wanted me. Wanted a life with me. All this time, when I hadn't so much as dared to let myself dream of the possibility of a future with him, when I had never let myself consider that he may see me as anything other than the strange girl next door, he had longed for that future.

And more than just wanting it...

You said you couldn't make her big. He had hurled those words accusingly at Uncle Stiltskin, not in a casual way. Not in the way I had taken it at the time, because he had wanted to be rid of his burden, but for this. For a future with me that I had never, in my wildest dreams, imagined him working toward.

Now Edrich was standing before me with features less guarded than I had ever seen them, waiting for an answer he clearly cared about. He had always been so competent, so sure, so unyielding, that it took me a moment to place his expression.

Uncertainty.

It was another stilted minute before I found my voice.

"Are you asking if I would have wanted to be with you, even if we couldn't... " I felt myself turn a bright, embarrassed fuchsia before I willed it away, fighting for the control I was only just getting a handle on. "Even if I couldn't have all of you?" I finished.

He swallowed, then nodded. I owed it to him to consider it seriously, so I forced myself to look away, to stop thinking of the way my hands itched to trace the rugged lines of his face again, and lower, to trail across his broad shoulders.

My skin slowly turned a shade of deep purple, and I looked back in time to catch Edrich's eyes stirring in response. Because he knew what that meant, he knew *me*. *And there's my answer.*

"That would have been enough for me. *You* would have been enough." I hadn't even finished my thought before Edrich was closing the short distance between us. He was in front of me with half a stride, his calloused hands cupping my face more gently than I would have thought possible from him.

"Lina," he breathed my name, but I didn't let him finish whatever he was going to say.

Because I may not have let myself think of the future, but I had spent half my life wondering what it would be like to have his perfectly shaped lips on mine. I erased the space between us. He opened his mouth to mine without hesitation, like he had been waiting as long as I had for this moment.

I knew, logically, that it was my first kiss, and it should feel awkward. But it didn't. It felt like my lips were made to be fused against his, like there was a wrongness in us being apart, and we were making it right with each searing point of contact.

His hands trailed down my shoulders, following the lines of my back and wrapping around my waist while I tangled my fingers in his shaggy blond hair. I had heard the girls at the tavern talk about stolen kisses, but I had never imagined that just the feeling of another person's mouth on yours could set your entire body on fire, make you feel safe and exhilarated and so many other conflicting feelings all at the same time.

I backed away enough to explore the hard lines of his chest, and I felt his fingers skate softly along the outside of my delicate wings. I shivered, and he smiled against my mouth.

When we finally, reluctantly, came up for air, he rested his forehead against mine.

"You should probably get back to your rooms in case they look for you in the morning." It was clear in his face that it was the last thing he wanted to be saying.

Logically, I knew he was right, but...

"Not yet," I said, fisting my hand in his shirt and pulling him back against me.

He chuckled against my lips, and the sound reverberated through every part of me. I pressed my palms against his chest, walking him backward toward the spacious four-poster bed.

He wasted no time in laying back, pulling me on top of him where my wings wouldn't be in the way. I had a split second to wonder what fairies did when both of them had wings before his next kiss chased away every rational thought.

After what felt like hours, Edrich propped himself up on one muscled arm.

"Fine," I preempted him when he sucked in a breath to speak. "You can walk me back to my rooms."

"Maybe just a few more minutes," he responded, leaning in for another kiss.

Eventually, though, I knew he was right. There might be a panic if they thought I was missing, so I reluctantly let him walk me down the two hallways, giggling and evading sentries as we went.

By the time we got to the door, I had finally braved myself to speak.

"Come with me," I breathed. This may be my only chance to sleep in his arms. "Just to sleep," I clarified, willing myself not to blush fuschia, again.

I heard him swallow before he held my gaze for a long moment, his cerulean eyes barely visible in the fading moonlight of the hallway windows. He opened his mouth, a begrudging refusal plain in his eyes, and I cut him off.

"You're leaving tomorrow, Edrich. I'm not ready to say goodbye... not yet."

"All right," he finally said.

This time, there was no awkwardness at all to sharing a room, a bed, a small pocket of space that only we existed in.

He rolled onto his back, holding out an arm for me, and it felt like the most natural thing in the world to press myself against his side, placing my head on his chest. His arm curved around me, never once struggling to find its place around my wings.

My mind raced.

Was it too much to hope that he might stay now? For that matter, was it too much to ask? He had a family, a band of mercenaries he was sworn to. *Wouldn't it be selfish to ask him to walk away from his life for mine?*

Something the prince said earlier came back to me.

Fate, he had mentioned.

I had never believed in it, really, and I still wasn't sure I did. But if the universe was willing to give me the gift of one beautiful night with the boy I had loved all my life, I wasn't about to turn it down.

48

EDRICH

It was nearly impossible to force myself to leave Lina before the sun came up. The sound of her soft breathing beckoned me back to bed, but I didn't want to risk Queen Cassia's disapproval by being discovered in her room—again.

Besides, Lina may not care about her reputation right now, but I didn't want to be responsible for her starting a scandal before she even settled in.

I spent a little extra time cleaning up and changing in my rooms, waiting for as long as I could before going back to her. We had spent years without this, whatever *this* was, but somehow it was impossible to imagine another moment without her in my arms.

Taking deep breaths, I continued to pace the floors of my suite, going over every possibility for what could happen next. My family would be well taken care of. They would be happy for me. *For us,* I amended.

A wave of doubt washed over me when I wondered if this was even something that Lina would want.

She was just barely starting her life here. *Would she really want me to stay and...*

I shook my head. After last night, I had to believe it's what she wanted, but she had also said pretty plainly that it was my last night here—had said it without a shadow of a doubt to her tone.

Either way, I wouldn't know until I talked to her. A glance at the clock had me cursing time for moving so slowly before my mind went back home.

Atesh would be understanding, if a little disappointed. But, weren't we both trying to leave that life behind? Didn't we both want to stop after the last mission?

Wringing my hands, I couldn't stop wondering how any of this was possible, or realizing how much of a fool I was for nearly not coming with her.

When a knock at the door sounded, I nearly ran to open it, surprising a servant with a breakfast tray. Thanking him, I moved the tray to the table, deciding to wait only a few more minutes before the rest of the palace was awake.

My stomach was a twisted vine of nerves as I thought about what I would say to Lina, how she would react.

I smoothed out my tunic and finally headed down the hall.

Aster's violet waves bounded into Lina's room just as I rounded the corner.

Excited voices floated down the hallway to me, and the corners of my lips tugged at Aster's infectious enthusiasm for life. Until I made sense of the words, and stopped dead in my tracks.

Because I had been wrong before, when I thought maybe this time, there was reason to hope.

I turned around, walking away from Lina's room, away from whatever ridiculous notions I had of spending my life with her.

49

LINA

Somewhere in the back of my sleepy mind, I expected to wake to the sound of Edrich's gruff morning voice, the one that warmed every part of me. Instead, it was Aster's bright tones that pulled me from sleep.

"Good morning, future sister-in-law!" she sang, just before the door clanged shut behind her. "I heard about Lark's proposal, in detail."

I shot her a wry look, still reeling with the way the bed was completely cold and empty aside from me. Where did Edrich go? *Does he regret last night, already?* Did he decide to leave early, or realize it was a mistake to allow ourselves to be so close if it was only going to end?

Does that mean there's no chance of him staying?

"All right, fine, I know you only said you'd think about it. And I'm sure you'll have to think pretty seriously, what with that sexy hunk of man-meat down the hall." She waggled her eyebrows, sinking onto the mattress next to me. "But I support you either way," Aster summed up, cheerfully.

Before I could say anything, she bounced up. "Oh, speaking of your companions, the other one found his way here this morning. He says he's your uncle, though I can't say I see a family resemblance…" she trailed off.

"Uncle Stiltskin is here?" I shot up, already looking for some clothes to throw on.

"Relax, Lina. You have time to eat and get dressed. He said he's getting washed up, and then I'll take you to meet him in the library."

I nodded mutely, my mind churning. Talking to Edrich would have to wait, I supposed, ignoring the sick, sinking feeling that gave me. Uncle was back, and he owed me an explanation.

❧ 50 ☙

EDRICH

I found myself back on the landing pad where Pepper had first brought me to this trolls-forsaken place.

Sister-in-law. Proposal.

All I could see was red.

Lina is going to marry the prince ... she's going to marry the prince and ... and I'm leaving.

Clenching my fists, I paced the landing pad, anger and humiliation rolling off of me in waves. My skin didn't need to change colors for the people around me to know how I was feeling. They all gave me a wide berth to stew in my miserable thoughts.

"You're leaving tomorrow." Her voice came back to me in an entirely new light. I had thought she was sad, maybe even tempted to ask me to stay. But in the cold light of day I saw it for what it was... a goodbye.

Son of a centaur.

I should have known better than to hope.

Unable to stand my own thoughts any longer, I took a

chance and whistled for Pepper. If she was nearby, maybe I would just go ahead and leave this place.

Pepper's cry alerted me to her presence just before she came plummeting toward me with a speed that was a little terrifying at my current size. She landed gracefully, though, immediately lowering her head for me to stroke her beak.

Already, it was easier to breathe. I had always preferred the outside air and the company of animals to people, the notable exception being... *No.* I refused to think about her right now. Not when she was probably thinking about her prince and the perfect future they would have together here.

Aster's words came back to mind, about why she had asked me to stay. I wondered if I was still honor-bound to even go to the ball, knowing that she didn't care for her own sake.

Though, I reflected again on how much bigger Pepper was than I was right now. *I can't very well leave like this.*

No sooner had the thought crossed my mind than an unwelcome grumble sounded from behind me.

"I thought I might find you out here."

I turned to see Rumplestiltskin standing with a corked glass bottle in his hand.

"If you're looking for another romantic hedgehog-back ride through the valley, I am sorry to disappoint." It was easier to joke with him now that my father's life wasn't hanging in the balance of every interaction we had.

Even if he is a scary little bastard.

Rumple's golden eyes crinkled in amusement before he laughed.

"No. I'm afraid I have other plans."

I nodded, stroking the feathers on Pepper's neck.

"The queen asked me to give this to you." He continued, before handing over the container full of ordinary-looking liquid. "If you want to get back to your regular size, that is."

The small vial felt like lead in my hand.

Hadn't I just been wanting this?

"Of course, I do," I said, automatically. "I have my family and my life to get back to. Why wouldn't I?"

"You tell me," he said.

"There's nothing to tell," I shot back, ignoring the slightly defensive note in my voice.

There *was* nothing to tell. Lina was making plans for a life here, a life I could never come close to giving her. Whatever happened last night was... nothing. *A goodbye... that's all.*

The little green man fixed me with a look that said I was unconscionably stupid to him, and I glared right back.

"Then off you go," he finally said. "No need to wait for the ball."

"I could hardly stand up my date," I said, with forced nonchalance. "Aster asked me to stay."

Rumple just shook his head, turning around, but not before I heard him mumble *"both a couple of idiots"* under his breath. Somehow, I knew the *'both'* wasn't referring to me and Aster.

He's talking about me and Lina.

I climbed atop Pepper and urged her to take off.

We had hours until the ball began, and I needed that time to collect my thoughts. I would say goodbye to Lina this time. *Even if it's for the last time.*

LINA

When I reached the study, my eyes roved over the endless shelves of books. Leather-bound tomes and novels lined every surface. Books filled with stories that I could devour in no time at all. I thought back to the books Mama and I had read together, at how much effort it took to read the pages so close up before turning to the next one, and the way she did it with such ease.

An unexpected pang darted through me at the memory. What I wouldn't give to have her read me a story one last time, to have her here to talk through some of this mess with.

I thought I would be angry when I faced Uncle again, but it was hard to hold on to that resentment as soon as I saw him.

He was sitting casually in an armchair next to a table, leafing through a book like it was the most natural thing in the world to him. And I didn't see the trickster or the man who had probably filled a lifetime with regrets. I just saw the man who had shown me nothing but love and acceptance and protection... even if he took that last one a little too far.

"Is Maggie all right?" It seemed like the safest subject to start with.

"I think she's disappointed that her toenail polish has chipped, but she's otherwise happy, down on the lower levels with the other hogs." His green lips stretched over his gold teeth, and I couldn't help a small answering grin.

It disappeared as soon as I took another look around, though.

"Why did you keep me from this place?" I asked, in a tired voice. I loved him, I did, but I had found a family here, and people like me.

"Lina, child." He motioned for me to take the chair across from him. "I wanted to save you from this."

I shook my head.

"There was nothing here to save me from. And again, *again*, why couldn't you have told me the truth and let me make that decision?"

"Things are much changed now from when your parents ruled. You had already lost so much. I didn't want to tarnish the memory or idea of who they were."

"Who they were... You mean dictators and warmongers —" I started, but he cut me off.

"No child deserves to carry the baggage of their parents, but neither were things that black and white. Your mother wanted you to be far away from all of this. She wanted a different life for you. And when war came, I had no choice but to take you from here."

"Right, because you owed her a favor. Why would you owe a favor to someone like that?" Emotion choked my voice, but I willed my colors to stay neutral.

Uncle winced, and I instantly regretted the words. He sighed and set his book down on the table beside him. Leaning forward, he spoke again, this time with a gentleness in his tone that he'd always saved just for me.

"Your mother wasn't all bad, Lina. She was just born into the wrong family, something I know about all too well."

I looked up at him, trying to parse the things I'd learned with the person I thought I knew.

"I owed her a favor, because she saved me." He said, stretching out his hand in question.

I glanced from it to his face before taking it. Once again, I was transported back in time.

Tendrils of fear crept up my spine as I stared back at the King of Ellaria. His aqua eyes were menacing, and his laugh was cruel as he ordered his guards to throw me into the dungeon.

Before they grabbed hold of me, I caught the eyes of the young princess, one with pointed, iridescent wings, watching me with a somber expression. Hyacinth. She held my gaze as they dragged me away.

Time skipped forward and I could feel the hunger gnawing at my—no, Uncle's—stomach. It had been days since he'd eaten. The smell of fear and death permeated the air all around him.

He was going to die here. He knew it.

Then, a small, cloaked figure appeared before him. When she spoke, her voice was like that of sunshine itself as she whispered assurances and frantically worked at the lock on the cell door.

The princess.

"Hurry. They'll be back any moment." Hyacinth wrestled Uncle's weak body up onto his feet.

Pain lined my vision and a small glimmer of the torture the guards had inflicted on him, slipped through. In spite of the damage done to his legs and feet, the dredges of hope flickered within him as an ember. Each step further from the cell fanned them into a flame until he couldn't feel the pain any longer. All that there was, was hope.

"We can escape through here." The princess whispered, pointing toward a side door of the prison. Just outside, two ravens rested on the ground, saddled and packed with supplies. Another prisoner rested on one of the birds with a female fairy sitting behind him keeping him steady.

Hyacinth wrestled Uncle onto the bird when alarm bells began to ring. The guard knew prisoners had escaped and it wouldn't be long before they found us.

Terror began to replace whatever hope Uncle had begun to feel, and Hyacinth could sense it.

She shook her head at the other fairy, and the female gasped, tears filling her eyes.

"I'll distract them, while you get away." The princess said, cutting off all protests from her friend. "Go. Take them far away from here."

I could feel Uncle's pulse racing through me. And a warmth spreading over him as he made a vow.

"I owe you a debt." His raspy voice came from my lips just as the ravens took off for the canopy above.

The world rushed around me until I was back in the room with Uncle, once again, sitting in front of me.

My cheeks were wet, and it took me a moment to realize it was because I had been crying.

"She sacrificed her freedom for my life, and that is a debt I will never be able to repay." The truth of his words was reflected in the emotion in his eyes.

"Regardless of who I am and what I've done, I always

keep my promises. But more than that, protecting you was something I wanted to do."

I looked away from the sincerity in his eyes and thought about the memory he'd shared with me in the forest. Everything he had ever done was to keep me safe. And I knew he cared. I had felt it. I had felt his emotions when he had held me as a baby, when he gave me to Mama. When he had checked in on me through the years. I knew better than to doubt his love for me. Underneath his scaled exterior, there was a good man.

One who sometimes went to extremes for the people he loved.

"I have made many mistakes in my life, Lina. But keeping you safe was never one of them. I'm just sorry I didn't do a better job."

Another tear slipped down my cheek, and I leaned over to grab his hand, once again.

"You did just fine, Uncle," I added, after a moment.

He cleared his throat and patted my hand.

"So, the farm boy made it here safely." He quirked an eyebrow.

"He did," I responded quickly.

Uncle nodded in some sort of understanding before adding, "He's worth more than I gave him credit for."

I smoothed out the skirts on my dress, fiddling with one of the flowers on the hem, trying not to revisit all the reasons Edrich might have left this morning without a word.

"Careful, Uncle. It almost sounds like you approve of him."

Rumple snorted and sat back, picking up a cup of tea.

"I wouldn't go that far," he grumbled, but his lips just barely tilted up.

At least I can take comfort in my family, both the new one I have discovered and the one that has been with me all along.

I COULDN'T FIND EDRICH. He wasn't in his rooms, and no one seemed to know where he went. Uncle said he saw him out by Pepper earlier, and some part of me worried he had decided to leave without saying goodbye.

He was honorable, though, whatever he thought of himself, and I was sure he wouldn't just stand Aster up. I couldn't disappoint my new family by missing this ball, so I reluctantly trudged back to my room to get dressed.

I had barely been in there for more than a few minutes before the door swung open and Aster barreled in, holding a large case with several other fairies behind her. Each of them was carrying stacks of ornate gowns with accessories and shoes on top.

"Lina, these are the royal dressers. I thought we might get ready for the evening together?" She smiled, and I found myself returning it.

"Sure, that would be nice," I answered, forcing my skin to stay neutral and not dip back to the blue it had been since I'd entered my room.

Aster must've caught on, anyway.

"What is this?" she asked, setting down the case and coming over to grab my hands. "Tonight is supposed to be a celebration."

She glanced back at one of the fairies with long green and silver wings like a dragonfly with emerald hair to match. The girl nodded and left the room, returning a few minutes later with two bottles and two glasses.

The girl popped the cork, and I registered that the drink must be champagne.

"Here. Drink this down, and then the girls will start on our hair and nails." Aster grinned and drank the contents of her glass quickly, before pouring herself some more. "I could get used to this, you know."

I finished my glass, as well, and took a moment to savor the sweet and sparkling pink liquid. It was similar to the champagne I had tried at The Poisoned Apple before—but also a thousand times more delicious.

I eagerly held my glass out for more and nodded my head.

"I could get used to this, too." I said, trying to banish the worry for Edrich from my thoughts.

Aster laughed.

"Everyone could use more fairy wine. But I meant that I could get used to having you around. I never met my sister, and I think it would've been wonderful to have grown up with one."

I stilled, the glass flute barely touching my lips before I pulled it away.

She hadn't met her sister because of the war. *Because of my parents.*

"Why are you so kind to me? After all of the hurt my family has caused you?" The question escaped me before I could help myself, but Aster didn't hesitate to respond.

"Because, for better or for worse, we are not our parents. It isn't your fault, what happened. So why wouldn't I show you kindness?" She stared at me with that intense violet gaze of hers, like it was the simplest explanation in the world.

I finished off my second glass and sat down.

"I just feel like this is too easy. Like everything is happening too fast and I'm trying to keep up or wait for the other shoe to drop... I'm sure I'm not making much sense. But, I just don't feel like I deserve any of this."

Aster set her glass down and knelt in front of me.

"Lina. Not every story has a terrible ending. Sometimes, tragedy is the beginning, and sometimes, there are even happily-ever-afters." She smiled, and I found myself wanting to return it. "If it would help, I could be a little meaner to you. Call you names and take away your booze."

I couldn't help but laugh at that.

"No, no. You can leave the booze. I think I may need it for tonight." I greedily moved my glass away from her reach.

"Suit yourself. But don't say I didn't offer," she added, with a wink.

The other fairies had remained distant while we'd talked, but suddenly one with orange wings like a monarch butterfly, stepped forward.

"Your Highnesses, if you please. We need to hurry, or you'll be late for the ball."

"All right, Fauna. Come work your magic and make us presentable." Aster threw a hand over her head dramatically, and the girls around us snickered.

For the next three hours we were painted, and brushed and primped and combed, then finally, dressed.

"Are you sure about this?" I asked, studying the ornate gown that had been chosen for me.

"Of course. You look stunning, Lina." Aster gaped and flitted around me in a slow circle.

I took in my reflection, barely recognizing myself. The dress was ivory and beige with sheer sleeves that cinched at my wrists, and a plunging neckline with intricate white leaves that were sewn into the otherwise sheer fabric.

It was all gossamer and silk, and easily the most beautiful thing I'd ever seen. Clove, the fairy with the dragonfly wings, brought over a small box, and Aster grinned wickedly when she opened it.

"This one is for me," she said, placing a golden tiara on her head. A large sapphire that matched the deep blues of her dress hung from the center and rested between her brows. It was stunning.

Then, she turned to me.

"And this one is for you."

My mouth dropped open. She'd given me tiaras to wear while I'd been here, but none so beautiful as this.

It was the same style, but made of silver with small, sparkling diamonds covering the metal, and, in the center, there was a teardrop-shaped pearl. She gently placed it on my head and stood back to look at our reflections in the mirror.

"Yes. I think we will do just fine this evening."

I shook my head.

"This is all too much, Ast—" I began, but she interrupted.

"Listen. In here, you are Lina, and that's great. We always want you to be yourself. But you are also Ixia... the famed lost princess, and there is nothing wrong with looking the part." She exaggerated the word *famed*, and I rolled my eyes.

I looked at myself in the mirror again. Trying to reconcile the things she said with everything I had learned over the past few days. With the memories Uncle had shared with me. With the life I knew on the farm. With the person I was at the tavern with my friends. And with the reflection staring back at me.

How is it possible to be both a princess and a girl from a simple village from the middle of nowhere?

As my thoughts swirled, the one image that kept coming back to mind, that kept interrupting every thought I had, that insisted on plaguing me even when I tried to push him away.

Edrich's face as he slept next to me.

The way his eyes closed as he leaned in to kiss me for the first time. My empty bed this morning. The way he was nowhere to be found, all day.

I wondered if the problem was that he didn't want to feel torn between lives. Could I go back with him? Even if that meant that he would take the tonic and return to his normal size. I'd meant it when I'd told him I would've chosen a life with him, even if it was only half a life. *Even if we can never really be together, my heart belongs to him and has since we were younger.*

Aster sighed next to me, and I looked up to see her brows furrow while she looked at me, as if she were reading my mind.

"Your colors give you away every time. You know that?" Then, she wrapped her arms around me and placed a kiss on my cheek. "I may not know every thought that was just flitting through your head just now, but I will tell you this. No matter what you choose tonight, I've claimed you as my sister, and don't plan to take that back."

I squeezed her tighter to me, and realized it would break something inside of me to walk away from all of them, from hugs like this and sisters like her.

"Thank you."

She let go and smoothed out her dress.

"I suppose we've made them all wait long enough," she added, with a wicked grin. "I'll meet you in the ballroom in five minutes. It's time to go break some hearts."

I wasn't sure who she was referring to, but I was pretty sure there would be plenty of broken hearts to go around.

❧ 52 ❧

EDRICH

Flying with Pepper had calmed me down just enough to know what I had to do. Say goodbye to Lina. Find a way to move on with my life.

Aster came to get me herself when it was time to head to the ball.

"Quite the gentleman," I joked.

"It doesn't hurt for you to make a pointed entrance." She shrugged.

I didn't have to wonder long what she was talking about, as heads turned to follow us down the hall. To follow me, or more accurately, to note my lack of wings in muttered, disdainful tones.

Then, Aster would shoot them a venom-coated smile, and they would quickly find themselves occupied with a different topic of conversation.

"I'm sorry," she said under her breath. "There's no excuse for their ignorance."

"Don't worry about it," I assured her. "It won't matter after today, anyway."

She stopped, then, just outside of the ballroom, and turned to look at me.

"I hope you don't mean that," she said, the sincerity in her tone taking me off guard.

"Why would you want me to stay, when—" I couldn't quite finish my thought, but she smiled anyway.

"I'm so grateful Lina was brought into our lives, but I'm not selfish enough to want to keep her here if it makes her miserable."

"She doesn't seem too miserable to me," I said. Though, even as I said it, I remembered the way she had stood defeated in her bedroom before I let her know I was there. I never had gotten to ask her about that.

There are plenty of things I haven't asked her about, though.

"That's what I thought," Aster said, examining my features. Then, her expression brightened into something mischievous. "Come on, now. Time for me to enter the ballroom with a tiny human on my arm. It's hardly an event if I don't make some kind of stir."

I couldn't help but smile back at her. That was the worst part, really, that I understood why Lina would want to marry into this family, to marry a prince.

That didn't make it any easier when Aster pulled me directly over to her family when we entered the room. I had never been to a ball before, but I was reluctantly impressed with the way the room combined opulence and warmth, weaving in sparkling streamers and glowing lanterns and pieces of nature to look like... well, like a fairy kingdom, I supposed.

It was easier to focus on that than the three people in front of me. Lina didn't seem to be here yet, which was a small mercy. I didn't feel prepared to look at her yet.

"It's good to see you again," the queen said, with a bit of a smirk, like she wanted to add, *and fully dressed this time*.

"So, this is the friend of the girl I've heard so much about," the king said, in a voice that was gruff, but not unkind.

At least, I assumed he was the king by the ornate crown he wore, gold leaves and branches with ruby roses set into it.

"This is Edrich," Aster confirmed. "Edrich, this is my father, and my brother, Larkspur."

"Lark," the prince corrected, congenially.

I was finally forced to turn my attention to the man I wanted desperately to hate, but as soon as I saw him, I knew that was impossible. He had a kind, open face, not unlike his sister's, and the smile he gave me was genuine.

Somehow, that makes it all worse.

I managed to dredge up a smile of my own, one that wasn't half as real as *Lark's*. Commotion behind me saved me from further attempts at conversation.

As soon as I turned around, I reconsidered that thought.

Because seeing Lina like this wasn't necessarily a better alternative.

She had always been gorgeous, but this was something else entirely. I was unprepared for how utterly breathtaking she looked walking into the ballroom.

I wasn't the only one who thought so. Heads turned to look at the newest addition to Ellaria as she practically floated across the gleaming wooden floor. She wore a pale, silky gown, and her hair was arranged around a tiara with a pearl the same subtle shades as her delicate wings. Her teal eyes were wide and sparkling, but they weren't taking in the enchanting ballroom like I expected them to be.

They were fixated firmly on me.

And I couldn't look away, even though I knew I should.

Aster cleared her throat as Lina came closer.

"I hate to ditch you so early, Edrich," she said. "But it's tradition for the ball to open up with a dance between my parents and one between my brother and me."

I tore my eyes away from Lina long enough to see confusion clouding the prince's eyes, and I reconsidered my thought that Aster was guileless. There was no time to call her on it, though.

The king raised his glass for an announcement, and the room went still.

"Tonight, we celebrate many things. One of our own has returned to us." He gestured to Lina, the glint in his eyes unmistakable. She was not the enemy and would not be treated as such. My respect for the royal family seemed to rise with each move they made.

"We have the rare honor of a human guest." He tilted his head in my direction, again making his intent clear. "And as most of you are aware, the reason we are all gathered here this evening. My son will choose his bride before dawn."

I hardly had time to process that before the queen declared the celebration officially starting, and the music began to play.

The four of them swept away to the dance floor, leaving me and Lina standing at the edge of the room by ourselves.

It seemed like the first dance was a standard beginning to these things, because none of the fairies hesitated before they coupled up and joined the monarchs on the dance floor. Lina and I stood only inches apart, tension zapping between us.

I was afraid to look at her again, afraid I would get lost in her ocean eyes and say something else to make an ass of myself when we had even less time than I thought we did, and her choice here was clear.

I couldn't take this opportunity from her when I had nothing better to offer. The best thing for me to do now was walk away before it got any harder on either of us.

Then I saw a handsome fairy approaching with his eyes on her, and I lost what little self-control I had.

Turning to her, I held my hand out.

"One last dance?" I rasped out.

It wouldn't be our first dance, not exactly. When we were kids, one of her many make-believe games had been, ironically enough, prince and princess. She would insist that I hold her in my hand and spin around the room with her until we were both dizzy.

And, of course, I obliged her, as much an idiot then where she was concerned as I am now.

But it would be our first dance like this, and I both craved that closeness and hated how hard it would be to walk away from.

Her eyes widened, and blue flashed over her skin before she took a deep breath, willing herself back to rose-gold.

"That's new," I commented.

"Aster taught me," she said, still looking at my outstretched hand.

I was about to pull it back to my side when she grabbed it, pulling me to the dance floor before I could rescind my offer. It was bittersweet, having her back in my arms and feeling like she belonged there, when I knew our time together was so short.

We glided around the room wordlessly, her eyes searching my expression for something before she finally spoke.

"Last dance? So you're leaving now, then?" Her inflection was so careful, almost distant.

"There wasn't much of a choice to be made," I said, carefully.

"I'm surprised you haven't left already." Her features were closed off, and I tried not to show how much the words stung.

"I left you once without saying goodbye. It wasn't a mistake I wanted to make again."

"And yet, that's what you did this morning."

I tried to decipher the anger in her tone, when she was the one who had spent the night in bed with me when she was engaged to another man.

"You can't expect me to stay when you're marrying someone else," I said, giving her more honesty than I strictly wanted to.

Her jaw dropped. "Edrich, I—"

The music cut off before she could finish her sentence, and I reluctantly stepped back.

"For what it's worth, Lina, I think you're doing the right thing."

Her lips parted in surprise, but she didn't correct me. Then Aster was there, tugging my arm.

"My turn," she practically sang.

My hands went to her waist automatically, hardly even

aware of what I was doing, because my attention was caught by the prince sweeping Lina away.

How appropriate.

Aster cleared her throat. "I thought, perhaps, you would prefer not to have that particular conversation in the middle of a bunch of gossiping fairies," she said under her breath.

"It's not a conversation I would prefer to have at all, actually." I still couldn't look at Aster because Lina was staring intently into Lark's face, her hand clutching his arm like he was a lifeline.

"But—" she started to respond, and I shook my head.

"My apologies, Princess, but I'm afraid I'll have to call it a night. I have an early start in the morning." I finally met her violet eyes to find them equal parts frustrated and sad.

That makes two of us.

"I wish you would stay and see this through." She shook her head, sadly.

I risked one last glance at Lina and Lark, still twirling in each other's arms and locked in some kind of serious conversation. *I know that if there is one thing in the world I'm not capable of, it's seeing another moment of this.*

"It's really better if I go." With that, I gave her a short, respectful bow, and walked out of the room with as much dignity as I could muster.

It was better this way.

❧ 53 ❧

LINA

Lark spun me in a slow circle as we kept pace with the other dancers on the floor. I was still reeling from what Edrich said. It didn't explain why he had left that morning, but at least I knew why he hadn't come back.

"I can see that when I asked if there was anything between you two, perhaps the answer was more complicated," he whispered, once I was facing him again.

I smiled up at him sadly.

"I'm sorry. Would you believe me if I told you that I didn't exactly know either? Not until last night, at least."

Lark chuckled under his breath and looked over at Aster and Edrich on the dance floor.

"I haven't known you long, but for some reason, I don't find that difficult to believe, at all."

"You're not... upset, then?" I hedged, afraid of what turning him down might make his family think of me.

The song ended, and we stopped moving. Lark held my

hands and looked me in the eye with a sincerity that was almost overwhelming.

"Not at all. Not ever, Lina. I meant what I said about your arrival. I think it would do the kingdom a lot of good for us to work together. But I would never make you stay. I would never ask you to sacrifice your happiness for a people you have only just met, and there are more ways to show an alliance than marriage." He pressed a gentle kiss to my knuckles and dipped his head. "I cannot speak for everyone, but as far as I am concerned, you are Ixia and this is your home, too. You don't need to be married to me to have a place in our family."

Tears stung my eyes at his kind words, and I gave him a small curtsy.

"Thank you," I told him sincerely, as I raised up on my tiptoes to place a kiss on his cheek. "Truly, thank you. I do still want to be a part of your family. I want to be your friend. But I gave my heart away a long time ago, and even if nothing comes of it, I wouldn't have felt right pretending otherwise."

He smiled and nodded.

"Do you know who you'll choose?" I asked.

"I have a fairly good idea... but I'm not sure it will be easy to get to her." He laughed and pointed behind me.

I turned around and was abruptly faced with a myriad of fairy women flocking toward the prince, shooting daggers at me with their sparkling eyes.

They were stunning, each in their own unique way.

But also, terrifying...

A few flashed hints of ruby under their skin as they looked me up and down, their irritation evident at my closeness to the man they were trying to woo.

I tried not to cringe as I took in others who displayed deep shades of purple skin as they stared at Lark. Knowing what triggered that color in me and knowing how they'd all been trained to control that better, it was easy to see that they were practically inviting the prince to strip them naked right here in the ballroom.

Gross.

Aster had been right. It was overwhelming to look at all of their emotions this way. My thoughts must've drawn her closer, because the next face I made out in the crowd was hers. She was looking back and forth between me and the door with a sadness in her eyes where I was now used to seeing mischief.

I made my way over to her and my heart immediately sank.

"Where's Edrich?" I asked, glancing around the room for him.

Her brows furrowed.

"He—he left. He seemed to think that you were going to take Lark up on his offer."

"What?" My chest felt too tight with all the things I hadn't gotten to say to him. "When?"

"A few minutes ago—" she started, but I didn't stay to hear the rest.

Panic gripped me as I made my way through the twirling fairies on the dance floor, pushing past the dining tables and lavish decorations. One thought lingered in my mind as I raced out the doors and down the hall, having no clue which direction he'd gone in.

I need to find him. I need to tell him the truth.

I raced down the corridor and toward my room, praying that he would still be there, that maybe he planned to change out of his suit before leaving. That maybe, somehow, he'd be waiting for me there. To say goodbye, to change his mind. To give me a chance to explain. *Anything.*

What if he's already gone?

If I had to go after him, chase him through the Enchanted Forest, I would.

I had to believe there was still time to fix this.

54

EDRICH

I was already in my room, halfway through pulling my bowtie off, when something Lina said the night before stopped me short.

Didn't you think I deserved a say?

Sure, she hadn't told me about her engagement... I told her I didn't want to make the same mistakes again, to choose for her. *But, isn't that exactly what I'm doing?*

Was it fair for me to decide what was best for her without even giving her all the facts? I couldn't give her the life the prince could, but didn't she get to make that call?

If I left now, I would be every bit the idiot Rumplestiltskin thought I was.

Am I really too much of a coward to risk my damned pride by telling her the truth before I give her up forever?

With that thought, I pulled my bowtie back in place and ripped open the door, prepared to sprint the short distance to the ballroom if I had to. Caught up in my thoughts and my hurry, I stepped out into the hallway just in time to plow into another, smaller person.

Lina.

She looked as frantic as I felt, but it was hard to form words now that she was standing right in front of me.

"Edrich." Her voice cracked as she said my name, staring up at me with expectant eyes.

She inched closer, her expression unsure as her fingers slid up the lapel of my tuxedo. She was so close I could smell the honeysuckle and lavender scent of her hair.

Before I could help myself, I leaned down, slowly, my nose brushing against hers in a silent question.

She exhaled a heady aroma of strawberries and champagne, and all I could think about was how much I wanted to kiss her.

My lips brushed against hers and she didn't back away.

"Don't marry the prince." I whispered against her mouth.

She hesitated, for the slightest moment, before pulling her eyes to mine, and shaking her head ever so slightly.

"I don't want him, Edrich. I want you. *Only* you."

Grabbing the lapels of my jacket, she pulled me the fraction of an inch closer, completely erasing the space between us.

Energy bolted between us like a frenzied storm when her lips moved against mine. Her teeth grazed my bottom lip, sending a bolt of lightning right through me. I didn't want to pull away, but I had to. *I need to know that this is real.*

"You're absolutely sure?" I asked, breaking the connection between us, pressing my forehead to hers.

"Edrich, when he asked me that, I thought... I thought

I would never see you again. I thought you would be okay with that, and that you were happy to be rid of me. And even then, I couldn't quite bring myself to say yes. Not when I knew that I had already given away the part of me that could love someone like that."

I started to talk, but she held a hand up.

"But, I also know that I can't ask you to stay this size, to give up your future for me. If we have to make it work, both of us our normal sizes, I would still rather be with you. Forever. In whatever way that has to be." Her breath caught, but she forced herself to continue. "You are my best friend, and that can be enough. Tell me that can be enough."

"No, Lina. It's not enough," I began, stunned. "I have loved you for as long as I can remember. I spent half my life wishing for a way for us to be together, and there is no part of me willing to give it up now that it's here." I stepped closer, my voice lowering as my heart hammered within my chest. "You *are* my future, the only one I care about."

Lina's eyes widened, her mouth parting slightly as she took a step closer, as well.

"I walked away from you once and it almost killed me," I said, closing the distance between us. "I'm not going anywhere this time, not unless you want me to."

"I don't want you to," she said breathlessly, looking up at me, her hands resting on my chest. "But what about your family?"

"We can still go back and see them."

"What about your job?" Her face darkened on that one. "What about—"

I cut off her question with another kiss.

"All that matters right now, is this." I added after a moment.

She smiled and leaned forward again, brushing her lips against mine before I stopped her.

"There is one condition, however..."

Her brow raised in question.

"Promise me that I don't have to call Rumplestiltskin 'Uncle'."

Lina's soft laugh was intoxicating.

"I'm fairly certain he wouldn't appreciate that." She smiled, before closing the distance between us once again.

Our first kisses had been tinged with regret for the time we had lost, and all of our uncertainty about the future. This one, though—it was full of hope and life and endless possibilities.

It was everything.

EPILOGUE
LINA

I t had been three months since we had walked through the doors of The Poisoned Apple. Three months of me getting to know my new family and kingdom while Edrich learned everything he could about animal medicine.

In spite of the letters we had sent back here, though, nothing had been able to prepare our friends for the sight of Edrich and I walking through the tavern doors.

Piper laughed outright, and Neira launched into asking me a million questions about my wings, and about Ellaria, and about my stunning golden wedding band with diamond dust in the center.

Vale was the only one who didn't seem to skip a beat, sliding two apple ales across the bar before we even made our way up there. Atesh poked and prodded Edrich like he was making sure what he saw was real, while Edrich swatted his hand away.

Only half an hour later, my *husband* was already tipsy

from trying to match me, ale for ale, but I was clear as the afternoon sun while I came to the end of our tale.

"Cassia and Aster created the world's most beautiful ceremony for us that week," I heard the words floating from my lips, barely able to believe the truth of them. That this was my life now, with Edrich and a family and a world that was my size. *That I have everything I've ever wanted.*

The only thing missing was Mama, but at least I could take comfort in the years I had spent being raised by the kindest, most nurturing woman even Uncle Stiltskin had ever met.

"I'm so happy for you, Lina—err—Ixia," Piper said, raising her glass to me.

It felt good to see my friends again, to be with them back in our tavern.

While I was in Ellaria, learning about my history and helping to bridge the gap in the kingdom, Piper and Neira had their own adventures and heartache, too.

I could see it in their eyes. The way these months had changed them—changed all of us.

But those are stories for a different time.

A MESSAGE FROM US

We need your help!

Did you know that authors, in particular indie authors like us, make their living on reviews? If you liked this book, or even if you didn't, please take a moment to let people know on Amazon, Goodreads, and/or Bookbub!

Remember, reviews don't have to be long. It can be as simple as a star rating and an: 'I loved it!'

So please, take a moment to let us know what you think. We depend on your feedback!

Now that that's out of the way, if you want to come shenanigate with us, rant and rave about these books and others, get access to awesome giveaways, exclusive content and some pretty ridiculous live videos, come join us on Facebook here: https://www.facebook.com/groups/driftersandwanderers

For even more freebies and some behind-the-scenes content, you can also sign up for Robin's newsletter here: https://www.subscribepage.com/robindmahlenewsletter_tse

ELLE'S ACKNOWLEDGMENTS

First and foremost I want to thank the peanut-butter to my jelly, the ice cream to my apple pie (don't tell Mammam) and my best friend Robin.

This project was it's own sort of adventure and I am so happy with the end result! Also, this is our eighth project together!! Can you believe it? (I mean, I can't imagine being able to convince you to write a Thumbelina retelling three years ago... but here we are! lol) It never ceases to amaze me how talented and witty you are. You bring such life into our characters and worlds and I am so grateful to be a part of this team! I can't wait to see else we will come up with together.

Jamie - I cannot put into words how much I adore you. You make every project better and I am forever grateful for your input and insights!

Rachel - Thank you for all of your help!! Lina and Edrich's story would not be what it is without your help!

Lissa - As always, thank you so much for adopting us at the release of our very first book. You have been and always will be invaluable to our team and us as a duo. We adore you and your feedback on each of our projects. Thank you for being a constant source of support and encouragement even on the days where creativity is lacking for us.

Jill - What would I ever do without you? You have been in my corner since day one and I love you to the moon and back! Thank you for believing in me, for being my friend and for all of your continued support. I am so fortunate to have you in my life and can only hope that everyone has a *Jill* in their corner.

To our Drifters and Wanderers reader group and our ElBin street team - thank you so very much for supporting us and helping us continue on in our author journey! We live for your posts and our interactions and want to thank you for helping us choose to write about Thumbelina as well as voting on the title. You guys are the best readers we could ask for. <3

To my hubby - Thank you for your constant love and support for helping with the kids when I'm on a deadline. Thank you for loving me through thick and thin, for being patient and forgiving, for helping me when I'm braindead and for always making me laugh when I'm stressed.

I love you more than Lina loves apple pie. You are my best friend and the mate to my soul.

And to all of our friends and family and readers and to everyone who picked up this book and gave us a chance -

thank you, thank you, thank you. You make it possible for us to keep writing. <3

ROBIN'S ACKNOWLEDGMENTS

First of all, a huge thank you to my bestie and co-author. It never would have occurred to me to write a Thumbelina retelling without your fairy inspiration. <3 Every book we write together manages to surprise me, and Promises and Pixie Dust was no exception! I can't wait to dive back into the Enchanted Forest with you to see what other stories it holds.

Thank you to Jamie, for dealing with our insane schedule and loving this book even before we did!

Rachel, I am ever grateful for your eagle eye and hilarious commentary. I hope you continue to lend us both!

Lissa, your feedback helped so much, and even managed to dial back some of the hate that came Edrich's way. Have I told you lately how much I appreciate your unending support?

To ElBin's Street Team, our awesome Drifters and Wanderers, and all the readers that gotten lost in our stories with us, we really wouldn't be writing at all without you. Your reviews, comments, and even just day to day engagement and camaraderie seriously make being an author worthwhile. <3

And as always, my first co-author, my ultimate best friend, and my husband. You are the actual best for staying up late so we had time to binge watch anime even around an insane deadline schedule, for being the most involved dad of all time, and most of all, for making sure I don't starve to death when I'm locked away in my writing cave. I couldn't do this without you (and wouldn't have ever started.)

I know I always forget someone, probably several some-ones, because so many people go into the process of making every single book. I appreciate all of it, though, even when my brain doesn't work well enough to remember things!

ABOUT THE AUTHORS

Elle and Robin are best-friends turned co-authors and this is their seventh book together.

The duo can usually be found on road trips around the US haunting taco-festivals and taking selfies with unsuspecting Spice Girls impersonators.

Elle and Robin have a combined PH.D in Faery Folklore and keep a romance advice column under a British pen-name for raccoons.

They have a rare blood type made up solely of red wine and can only write books while under the influence of the full moon after sacrificing brownie batter to the pits of their stomachs.

And somewhere between their busy schedules, they still find time to create words and put them into books.

f

ALSO BY ELLE AND ROBIN

Our very first series is finished and ready to binge read here:

Winter's Captive

Spring's Rising

Summer's Rebellion

Autumn's Reign

The Lochlann Treaty

Twisted Pages Series:

Of Thorns and Beauty

Of Beasts and Vengeance

Coming Soon:

Of Glass and Ashes

And finally, the reason this whole journey started...

Robin D. Mahle began as a husband and wife team to create Clark and Addie and their amazing story.

Check out the completed series here:

The World Apart

Made in United States
Troutdale, OR
07/06/2024

21063674R00202